Love THE ONE you're with

USA TODAY BESTSELLING AUTHOR
JENNIFER PEEL

Dedication

TO ANDREA AND EMILY, THANK YOU FOR YOUR
FANTASTIC STORIES ABOUT *SPYING* AND FOR MAKING
ME LAUGH UNTIL MY SIDES HURT.

Prologue

"I LOVE YOU, DADDY," Maribelle said through her sniffles while she tightly squeezed the man in our lives.

"I love you more, darlin'." Jake held on with an iron grip. "Do me proud, baby girl. Don't let this opportunity pass you by like I did."

I grabbed my midsection, feeling the sucker punch of his words. I knew the life Jake and I had made together wasn't his first choice, but to hear him verbalize it, especially after over seventeen years of marriage, killed me. The life we had built was all I'd ever wanted, mostly.

"Save some of that hugging for me." I plastered a fake smile on my face. Don't get me wrong, I was happy to see my baby spread her wings. But how was she old enough to be going to college? And what did it mean for me and her daddy? Something between me and Jake had changed over the last couple of years. And if I was being honest, I was a little worried.

Jake kissed Maribelle's tear-stained cheek before stepping away to let me have at her. Before wrapping my arms around her, I stared at her in disbelief. It wasn't like I hadn't already memorized how beautiful she was, from the naturally wavy strawberry blonde hair she'd inherited from me, to her daddy's blue-as-the-sky eyes that shone with such goodness and an excitement for life. I had even memorized each little freckle on her cute button nose. She was perfect. I never seemed to get enough time taking in her beautiful face.

"Momma," she cried before flinging herself into my arms.

I clung to her like I had the first moment the labor and delivery nurse had laid her, wailing like a tornado siren, in my arms. From that first touch, I knew that no matter how people judged me for having her at all of eighteen years old and *trapping* Jake into marrying me, I could face the world with my head held high, because she would need me to. Her feisty spirit gave me the courage to hold on tight for the ride that was called motherhood. Now it was giving me the courage to let go. To watch her take this next step in life.

"My Maribelle, I love you so much." The tears I'd been holding back began to trickle down my face and land on her shoulder. She had surpassed my five-foot-five frame a good four years ago now. Thankfully, she had gotten her daddy's height.

Maribelle shook in my arms, which surprised me. She'd been telling me since she was ten years old that she couldn't wait to move out and go to college. In her even younger years, each time she'd gotten mad at me she'd pack her suitcase and start walking to either Jake's parents' or mine. At four years old, she'd demanded to go to kindergarten. Like I said, she was a feisty one. It made her trepidation now harder on my heart. She broke it in two when she whispered, "If you let me come home now, I will."

Oh goodness. I wanted to let go of her and start throwing her clothes back in her suitcases. Instead, I leaned back and wiped some tears off her smooth, creamy cheek. "My darling girl, I believe in you. You are going to do amazing things this year. And I will always be here for you, whether you are flying or falling. I'm going to cheer you on when you soar and cheer louder for you when you stumble and fall, because I know you'll always get back up and try again. So as much as I want to take you home right now, I can't do that. You have a lot of flying to do this year. But I promise, I'm only a phone call away. Or a four-hour drive. Unless your daddy's driving—then it will be more like three."

Maribelle giggled while looking around her dorm room, decorated to the nines in shades of pink and gray. Lights strung from end to end. Not to mention a cream shag rug that looked as if we'd skinned a giant Persian cat. To say she was spoiled was an understatement.

Maribelle bit her lip. "Well, I would hate to waste all your decorating skills."

"It would be a shame. And if you came home, I would have to return that new fall wardrobe you just had to have."

"Those knee-high leather boots alone are worth staying for."

"That's my girl." We loved our shoes.

She took a deep breath and a step back. "I can do this."

"I know you can." The question was, could I? I looked at Jake, hoping for a hand to hold, but he was gazing longingly out the window at the courtyard below. He was running his hand through his thick dark hair that had the perfect amount of curl. Perhaps his hairline was a tad off from where it used to be, though I wouldn't say that to him. Just like I wouldn't tell him he should probably give his belt a break and let it out a notch. He was still lean and trim, but nowhere near as skinny as he was in our high school days. Regardless, it didn't matter how time was treating him—he was still the most handsome man to me.

It had been his dream to study prelaw here at the University of Alabama. Instead he'd ended up changing diapers and doing two a.m. feedings. He'd had to take a job at his uncle's car dealership to support us. He never complained out loud, but his silence the last few years and his distance, at times, spoke volumes. Even now that he was the sales manager and making more money than we ever thought he would, he still didn't seem satisfied. I feared he would always feel like he had missed out.

"We should hit the road," Jake said more to himself than me.

I gave Maribelle another big hug. "I'm going to miss you more than a hot fudge sundae on a warm summer night," I choked out.

"I'm going to miss you more than Rhett," she sobbed.

Well, that was saying something. Rhett was her

high school boyfriend and she'd been head over heels for him since junior high. But Jake had made her break up with him halfway through her senior year. He was determined that she wasn't going to repeat history—our history.

"Okay, okay." Jake held open his arms, trying to stave off another argument about Rhett. Maribelle was still heartbroken over him. "Give your old man one more hug."

We were hardly old. We were probably the youngest parents on campus today, especially considering Maribelle was only seventeen.

Maribelle obeyed and snuggled against her daddy's chest. He held her tenderly, making my heart pitter-patter. Maybe Jake wasn't always as sensitive as I wished him to be, but he was a great daddy. Even when we were younger and had no clue what we were doing, he'd always given Maribelle his all. Me on the other hand . . . well, he tried.

"Be good." Jake reached into his pocket and pulled out a wad of cash. "This is for you."

"Thank you, Daddy." She kissed his cheek.

Jake placed his hand over where she'd kissed him, his eyes misting. "Call your momma every day."

"I will." She smiled at me.

Jake headed for the door. I supposed that was my cue.

"Bye, baby girl." I tried to swallow down my emotions and be brave, though what I really wanted to do was hold on to her legs like she used to do when she was no taller than Tom Thumb.

Maribelle must have had the same thought, as she

was gripping her bedpost, holding herself firmly in place. "Bye, Momma," her voice cracked.

"Come on, Kasie. She's going to be late for orientation." Jake opened the door.

I'd been hoping for a more affectionate response, but I should have known better. I nodded and followed him out, leaving a big piece of my heart behind. It was a silent walk back to his truck and for the first several minutes of our drive back home to Nashville. Back to where it had all started for us senior year, with the homecoming dance. I knew I wasn't the first girl he'd asked, but from then on, we were inseparable. Life after that night seemed to revolve around seeing Jake. Passions ran too high and inhibitions too low for seventeen-year-old kids. We'd skirted the edge too many times, and on Valentine's Day we'd ended up crossing it. We married right after graduation and in November of that same year we were blessed with Maribelle. I knew back then we shouldn't have played with fire, but right now I would give almost anything to feel the heat of those first days together, of our first time. The days where we were able to talk for hours on end.

I hated the silence and more than anything hoped it wasn't what we had to look forward to for the next fifty years together. The only sound that could be heard now was the radio. A song I'd always thought was depressing was playing—*If you can't be with the one you love, love the one you're with.* In the back of my mind I wondered if that was how Jake saw me. The one he had to love because he had no choice.

I took a deep breath and got a whiff of that new-truck smell. "Hey, Jake, I was thinking since we're empty nesters now, we should do something to celebrate. Maybe go to Disney World and take silly pictures to post on social media about how we're living it up now that we're alone."

Jake twisted his hands around the steering wheel. "You know how busy I am at work right now."

"Right. Well, then let's take swing dance lessons. There's a great dance studio downtown that your brother said we should check out. I think his latest girlfriend runs it, or maybe it's her cousin. I can never keep track of all his women." Dallas was Jake's older brother, but he acted younger. He was a professed ladies' man who swore he would never settle down. I adored him. He was the only person on Jake's side of the family, besides Jake, who didn't blame me for ruining Jake's life.

"Kasie," he sighed. "You know I hate that girlie stuff."

I leaned my head against the cool passenger window. "Or maybe you just hate me," I whispered.

The truck jerked, and Jake swore. "Why would you say something like that?"

I sat up and faced him. His eyes kept darting between me and the road.

"Jake, I know this isn't the life you dreamed of."

He gripped the steering wheel even tighter. "We've had a good life and raised a great kid."

That was all true. We'd fared better than anyone thought we would, but ... "This life wasn't your first choice. I wasn't even your first choice. I know you asked Vivian to homecoming first, and you only asked

7

me after she turned you down. Had she said yes, I wonder if we would be here right now." Unfortunately, I thought of Vivian way too much. The homecoming queen. The queen of real estate in Nashville. Billboards of her and her movie-star-gorgeous husband were plastered all over the city. Now she was going to be starring in some reality TV show that started in January—*Wives of Nashville.* That meant more billboards. I wondered if that was the life Jake wanted—two professionals living the high life. Instead, he was married to Suzy Homemaker. Sure, I had my own little online boutique where I sold mommy-and-me matching dresses and hair bows that I designed and sewed with the help of my best friend, Abilene. We made a fair amount of money, but it wasn't glamorous.

He rubbed the back of his neck. "Kasie, why are you bringing up the past? What's done is done."

"Is it?" my voice cracked. "Jake, I've always loved you. And for a long time, I thought you loved me too; but the last couple of years, I'm not so sure. Maybe now it's time I love you enough to let you go. Let you live the life you wanted to."

He whipped his head toward me with wide eyes. "Please stop talking like that. You're emotional because we just dropped off Maribelle."

"Maybe. But I don't want to live a lonely life with you. I want to be with someone who wants to go on adventures and wakes up every morning excited to spend another day with me. And I want to be with someone who . . . loves me."

"You know I love you, Kasie," he replied, half-exasperated.

"But you're not in love with me. At least, you aren't anymore. There's a big difference. And it doesn't seem to matter how hard I try, you don't love me like I love you. Maybe it's time I recognize that's probably never going to happen."

His splotchy red skin and silence said it all.

Tears poured down my cheeks. "I think we should face the truth," I stuttered, my heart breaking into a million pieces. "It's time to say goodbye."

Chapter One

Five Months Later

"YOU SHOULD HAVE WATCHED *Wives of Nashville* last night," Abilene, or Abs, as I called her, squealed like a woman much younger than her forty years. I could barely hear her over the hum of our dueling sewing machines in our small makeshift office at my momma's house. Abs was obsessed with the show that had captivated our fair city and the nation.

I let up off the foot pedal and wrinkled my nose.

"No thank you."

Not only did I not enjoy reality TV, but you couldn't pay me to watch Vivian Jennings and her husband, Beau, with their too-perfect smiles and bodies that looked like they were cut from fine marble. Though, I had heard a rumor on social media that they'd had a lot of plastic surgery done. Part of me really wanted to believe it, but the decent side of me said it was a shame that they felt like they had to alter their appearance. I mean, Vivian was my age—thirty-six. Regardless, I'd gotten enough of Vivian in high school to last me a lifetime. I swore she'd spent those entire four years trying to one-up me. I had no idea why. Her family came from the upper middle class; and, well, my family was on the low side of lower middle class. We'd had to make do with what we had, which was why I'd learned how to sew and gotten a job when I was fifteen. I'd paid for all my school and extracurricular fees—including being on the cheer squad, that of course Vivian was the captain of. I'd even made a lot of my own clothes. Vivian had made fun of them, yet on several occasions had tried to copy my style using name-brand pieces. She'd always been more popular and, admittedly, more beautiful than me. Yet she'd always made sure I knew my place. Even after she'd turned Jake down for homecoming, she made sure to rub it in that he'd asked her first.

Abs gave her machine a break too and leaned forward with a conspiratorial grin. I loved her. We'd been best friends since we met in the car line back when our girls were in second grade.

"Oh, you would have loved it. All the other wives think Vivian is a big fat fake even though she's an audience favorite. They're accusing her of being manipulative and making everything about her."

"Sounds about right."

Abs laughed. "There is definitely something off about her. She's sickly sweet but gives backhanded compliments and constantly corrects her castmates in the name of 'helping' them. Last night she told Pauline—her husband plays for the Titans—that if she got a boob reduction it would help her back problems and make her dresses fit better. She emphasized that last part in her sugary voice. If you ask me, she was calling her fat."

I had no doubt; I knew that voice all too well. I could still hear her saying, "Kasie, it's such a shame you can't afford cheerleading camps in the summer. I bet if you could, you would be head cheerleader instead of me. I'm honestly amazed Coach let you on the team. But good for you."

I hated that I was so intrigued, but I had to ask: "So what's the point of the show other than them dressing up in evening gowns and showing off their bursting to be free bustlines for the millions of bill-boards up and down I-65? Which are over the top, by the way. Who lounges around on chaises all day?"

Abs took a sip of her dirty Diet Coke. We called it our happy drink. "The point? I'm not sure there is one other than it shows you a good way not to live your life. Most of these chicks are crazy. We are talking hair pulling and slapping each other."

My eyes widened. "You're kidding. Has anyone slapped Vivian?" I asked with way too much hopeful-ness.

"Not yet, sugar, but it's still early in the season. Like I said, she's still playing the innocent victim. She goes home crying to her husband, Beau, every night, complaining about how awful and mean the other wives are while he drinks a bottle of bourbon. If you ask me, that marriage has some issues. Men don't drink like that for no reason. And I don't trust people who air kiss and call each other pookie bear. It's not natural."

She made me giggle. "Vivian isn't someone to

trust. You know she switched the ballots for home-coming queen? She took my name off them."

Abs slapped her chest. "Nooo!"

"Yes ma'am. Of course, she got away with it because the administrators couldn't believe perfect Vivian would ever do such a thing. They wouldn't even redo the election because they felt she would have won regardless."

"Now I hate her for real. I hope the other wives find a way to sabotage her."

"I won't hold my breath. She's like ice—cold and everything slides right off her."

"Karma is a nasty beast and always catches up to people. You'll see." She gave me a wink.

I think Vivian must have paid Karma off. She would forever be the queen. At least she never got Jake. Or maybe she did. I still wondered if Jake rued the day she said no and I said yes. He could be the king of real estate right now. I'd lost track of how many times he'd said, after seeing one of her billboards, "She's done well for herself. No surprise there, though."

Once upon a time he was happy with me, right? Sometimes I think our first few years together when Jake could never seem to get enough of me were a dream. There had been several tender moments throughout our marriage, they had just gotten fewer and fewer as the years went by. I knew he resented that he never got a college education, and working for family had its drawbacks. His uncle always expected him to work longer and harder than anyone else. Which isn't to say Jake wouldn't have anyway, but the pressure ate at him. Still does. And I think he feels trapped there. His uncle gave him a break when no one would, and as much as Jake would like to leave, he has always felt like he couldn't. The money was too good and the guilt too thick.

While I sewed and contemplated, a booming voice shook the house.

"Dallas is in the house!" rang through my momma's tiny one-story brick home.

I smiled at Abs.

Abs bit her lip. Her rosy cheeks said how excited she was to hear Dallas's voice. I'd warned her that he wasn't one to be tamed, but I think after she divorced her deadbeat husband last year, she was looking to be wild. Dallas fit the bill. He usually went for younger women though, and Abs was the same age as him. However, she didn't look a day over thirty with her gorgeous long auburn hair, smooth fair skin, and soulful brown eyes.

I pushed back from my sewing machine and stretched my back. I'd been working on a retro-style cocktail dress as a special order for a client. "I wonder what Dallas is doing here," I mused out loud. In my head I wished it were his brother even though I knew how unlikely that would be. After five months of separation, I was more and more convinced we were headed for divorce. Both of us were dragging our feet when it came to filing. I think he kept waiting for me to do it and I kept expecting him to. Wasn't that what he wanted?

I heard Dallas teasing my momma before he walked back. "Momma Jo, I'd marry you for your hot chicken and biscuits alone."

"Honey, you couldn't afford me. I married for love the first time, God rest Billy's soul. The next time I marry someone, it's going to be for their money." She was all talk. I didn't think she would every marry again. She loved Daddy too much.

Dallas's laugh carried like a megaphone. "Challenge accepted. I guess I better start playing the lottery," he teased her.

"Save your money and get yourself a good girl. It's about time you settled down," she admonished him.

"Nah. No fun in that."

I could picture Momma rolling her eyes. "I suppose you're here to see my daughter," she rebuked him with her annoyed voice. "She's in the back."

"Don't hate me because I'm beautiful." He tried working his way back into her good graces with humor.

From the way she laughed, I would say it worked.

Dallas's footfalls could be heard and felt as he walked down the hall to our cramped quarters. My sewing room at home, or what was once my home, was much bigger and more functional. Jake had built me some great shelves and cubbies for all my fabric. And the countertops he'd put in were glorious. He'd even custom built the long tables that were perfect for cutting fabric on. They were too big to bring along. And it didn't seem right. They were too much of a reminder of Jake. Not that I didn't think about him every minute of every day. At least it wasn't every second anymore.

Abs smoothed her hair before Dallas walked in looking like he owned the place in his dark suit. He was a financial manager for a digital wealth management company. You wouldn't know it by his boisterous attitude, but he was all business during the day and excellent at what he did. I knew Jake was jealous of him. Their parents didn't help any, either, always touting Dallas's credentials and degree. It was awful and ridiculous since Jake made as much or more than Dallas selling cars for a living. There was no shame in that.

"Little sister." Dallas came at me with his arms open wide.

I stood and let him wrap me up. He was a big man, even taller than Jake. Like his brother, he had dark hair, but his was slicked back with no curl. And he was getting a few strands of gray.

"How are you?" I said, muffled against his chest.

"I have a bone to pick with you."

I leaned back and looked into his hazel, mischief-filled eyes. "What did I do?"

Before he answered me, he looked over my head. "Hello, Miss Abilene," he drawled.

"Hello, Dallas," she practically whispered back. She always got so shy around him. Maybe it was because she thought they should at least date, given that they were both named after towns in Texas. It would be pretty cute, Abilene and Dallas. But I didn't want Dallas to break her heart. The Baldwin brothers were hard to get over. I wasn't sure I would ever get over Jake. Maybe if we got divorced, it would help. Though the thought hurt my heart something fierce.

"Now back to you, young lady."

I rolled my eyes. "You're only four years older than me."

"That's a lot more years of wisdom."

"Uh-huh." I wasn't buying it. "What do you want?"

"I don't want anything. However, I do *need* you to end this nonsense and go back to my brother."

I let out a heavy breath and took a seat. We'd had this conversation before, and I was tired of it. "Your brother knows where I'm at. If he wanted me to come home, he would have asked me himself."

He reached down and shook my shoulders. "Woman, can't you see the man is in misery? Show him some mercy, would you please?"

"He's doing fine on his own." It wasn't something I was exactly happy about, but it didn't surprise me either. I mean, sure, he'd seemed a little thinner when I saw him a few weeks ago at Christmas at Maribelle's begging that we all spend the holiday together. So, he might have inhaled an entire pan of my cinnamon rolls like he hadn't eaten in weeks. Other than that, he seemed . . . well, melancholy, but he wasn't an overtly emotional guy anyway. And holidays were never really his thing. The greatest effort he'd made was buying me gift cards, and when Maribelle was little, he would put together any toys or bikes that needed assembling. Beyond that, he pretty much left the holidays up to me. This past awkward Christmas was no different, other than that he had bought me extra gift cards.

"You know that's a lie, Kasie Ann Baldwin." He used my full name like I was in trouble. "He doesn't even want to watch the Super Bowl next weekend. You broke him, girl. Now fix him. While you're at it, I would appreciate it if you made your party spread for us like you do every year for the game. That seven-layer dip you make is worth some tears of joy, baby."

I narrowed my eyes at him. "Oh, I get it. You two only want me to cook for you. That's all I'm good for. Did Jake send you over here?" My voice cracked, so full of hurt.

"You better watch yourself," Abs warned Dallas.

Dallas cleared his throat and gave Abs a sheepish glance before he dropped to his knees so he could look me in the eyes. "Girl, don't cry." He rested his large hand on my cheek. "I swear Jake doesn't know I'm here."

I tried to turn from him, embarrassed, but he wasn't having it. He held my face firmly in his hands. "Listen here, you pretty little thing. You're the best thing that ever happened to my pigheaded brother. And I know you miss him as much as he misses you." His thumb swiped some of the tears off my cheek.

"He doesn't miss me. He doesn't even love me."

"The hell he doesn't. Every time I'm at your place, he won't so much as let me leave a cup on the coffee table. He's always saying, 'Kasie likes it this way,' or 'Don't touch that, it's Kasie's.' The man is treating your house like a Kasie shrine."

The thought that Jake may be missing me made my heart skip a few beats, but it seemed too good to be true. "Then why hasn't he asked me to come home? Or better yet, why didn't he ask me to stay?"

He let go of my cheeks and tapped my nose. "You don't know men very well. You wounded the darn fool's pride and called him out on his crap. Baldwin men don't exactly respond well to the truth sometimes. And the truth is, Jake knows he should have been a better husband."

I sniffled and wiped my eyes. "Did he say that?"

Dallas smirked. "Not in so many words. But all his moping and whining spells it out."

I sat up straighter. "I don't believe it. When I accused him of not being in love with me anymore, he didn't deny it. In fact, he didn't say anything."

"Kasie," Dallas's voice was as tender as I'd ever heard it. "Darlin', he had to become a man before he even understood what that was."

"He resents me for it. He resents that we got pregnant."

"No," Dallas adamantly said. "He loves that girl of yours, and he loves you. He just isn't good with words. I'll tell you this, though, he was so proud when he could finally afford to build you your dream home. I've never seen him smile so big as the day y'all moved in."

That had been a wonderful day four years ago. Jake had been unnaturally happy that day. We'd even made love that night on our bedroom floor among all the unpacked boxes. As I had lain in his arms afterward, with his hands gliding smoothly across my bare skin, he'd kept asking me if I loved the place. It was one of those times in our marriage when I'd felt as if he wanted me as much as I wanted him.

"While he doesn't have the words, he shows it in other ways," Dallas added.

"Not always. And even if that were true, I need the

words too," I cried. "If he really loved me, he'd find a way to say it."

Dallas sank to the floor. "I hope for his sake, the stubborn fool learns to open his mouth."

"I'm not counting on it," I sighed. Maybe it was time to hire a lawyer.

Chapter two

GOOD NIGHT, BABY GIRL. *I love you.* I sent my nightly text off to Maribelle while I organized the shipments that needed to go out the next day. If I got much busier, I was going to have to hire Abs on full time and get another part-time person. I wished I could hire Abs full time now so she didn't have to work nights as an assistant manager at a nearby hotel, but I wasn't quite there yet. Especially now that I was living the single life. Well, sort of. I looked down at my thin gold wedding band and tiny round-cut diamond. Jake had promised me the day he gave it to me that one day he would buy a bigger diamond. I'd told him I didn't want another ring, that his love was enough for me. Maybe I should have taken him up on it.

I twisted my band. I hadn't been able to take it off yet. It seemed so permanent. But it was probably ridiculous to hold on to any hope at this point. We'd been separated since August, and we were well into January.

I fell back on my bedroom floor, surrounded by shipping supplies and carefully folded dresses wrapped in tissue paper and stacked neatly in piles. Man, did I miss my house. But I couldn't stand feeling so alone there. It's why I'd moved out. I never thought I'd be back in my old cornflower blue room with its hand-painted sunflowers on the wall. Or sleeping on my old creaky twin bed that Jake and I—well, never mind. We were two stupid kids who thought they knew everything. That misconception was quickly corrected when Maribelle arrived all perfect at a whopping nine pounds. We had no idea what we were doing. Still, we'd all survived somehow.

My phone buzzed. I picked it up to see Maribelle's reply. *Love you. Did you talk to Daddy today?*

I hated what this was doing to Maribelle. She was beside herself about it, trying her best to help us kiss and make up. The amount of mistletoe she had hung up around the house during Christmas break was cute, but not useful. I was pretty sure Jake didn't even know what the stuff was. She'd also made us watch a montage of old family videos from holidays and her birthday parties. I had cried through the entire thing, mostly because I couldn't believe my baby was so big now, and also because there were moments where I could almost feel the love Jake and I had once shared. Tender times when Jake would wrap his arms around me from behind and whisper in my ear that I was a good momma and that he loved me.

I wiped a tear from the corner of my eye and texted back. *Not today.* Probably not tomorrow or the following days after that. Communication was never our strong suit. Besides, I figured he was happy I'd left.

However, after talking to Dallas I wasn't so sure. But if he was so miserable without me, why didn't he reach out?

Maribelle sent back the teardrop emoji. My guilt bubbled up inside. I went back to work, knowing it would be a long night and sleep wouldn't come easily. It hadn't in months. I missed the sound of Jake's steady breaths and the way his hand would rest on my hip as we slept. He wasn't a snuggler, but all I needed was his touch.

After ten, my phone buzzed again. I assumed it was Maribelle calling to beg me to call her daddy. I was more than surprised to see Jake's name on my screen. Maribelle must have gotten to him. The girl had him wrapped around her finger. For Christmas he'd bought her a car. The cashmere sweater and earrings I'd given her paled in comparison, but I knew Jake hadn't done it to one-up me. He was all about making Maribelle's dreams come true, and she'd been begging for her own car since she was sixteen.

With some trepidation and a pounding heart, I answered my phone. "Hello."

Jake cleared his throat. "Kasie?" It sounded like a question.

"It's me."

"I knew that," he tripped on his words. "Hi," he said nervously.

"Hi. What's up?" I tried to keep it casual.

"I was just going through the bills and balancing the household account and I saw a weird charge."

Oh. This wasn't an *I can't live without you* call.

"Well, I haven't used the account in a long time." I sighed.

"I know. Why is that?" He sounded upset by it, which surprised me.

"I'm getting by on what I'm making. Besides, it doesn't seem right to take your money under the circumstances."

"My money?" He sounded angrier. "When have I ever made you feel as if it were only my money?"

"Never. That was one thing you were always good about. You always made me feel like the money you made was ours."

"At least I was good at something," he grumbled.

I scooted back toward the wall to give my back some support. "I'm sorry if I upset you. What's the charge for?"

"Says, Swing Dance Nashville."

I smacked my forehead. "Shoot. That was me. I must have given them the wrong debit card. I'll put the money back in the account."

"That's not necessary. The money I make is *ours*."

Ours? Was there such a thing anymore? "You shouldn't have to pay for my hobby." It wasn't a hobby yet. My first lesson was in a few days. I'd been trying new things the last couple of months and dating myself. I had to say I was an excellent date. I'd taken myself to watercolor painting classes and karaoke night, where I sang myself the sweetest ballad. I'd also gone to art galleries and even ice skating. Seriously, I was the best date ever. I had to say, though, I did miss the good night kiss.

"I don't mind," he growled, sounding like he did

mind. "Who are you taking swing dancing lessons with?"

"No one."

"You're dancing by yourself?" He sounded relieved.

"Of course not," I laughed. "I'll get assigned a partner."

"A man?"

"Yes, a man."

"You're going to dance with some strange man? Do these places do background checks?" He was obviously unhappy.

"Jake, it's going to be fine. It's a reputable place. I'm not worried at all." In fact, I was excited about it. I'd always wanted to learn how to swing dance.

"Will he be touching you?"

I stifled my laugh. "That is how dancing works."

"I don't like it."

I put him on speaker and rested my head on my knees. "Why do you care, Jake?"

He paused for a moment. "You're my wife," he whispered.

"Am I?" My voice hitched.

"Last I checked."

That wasn't the answer I wanted—needed. "I'll let you go. It's getting late."

"What do you want from me?" he begged to know.

"What I've always wanted," my frustration came out. "I want to be your wife, not just the woman you're married to."

"Kasie, that makes no sense."

"Jake, it makes perfect sense. I haven't been your wife in a long time. I became the woman who made your dinner and cleaned the house."

"You make it sound like I treated you like my maid."

I sat back, letting my long, wavy hair out of its messy bun. It draped my face as it fell past my shoulders. "You didn't, but you haven't treated me like your wife, either, for a long time. I can't even remember the last time we went to bed at the same time. You'd rather watch sports. Or—"

"You used to like to watch them with me," he interrupted defensively. "What changed?"

"Oh, I don't know. Your comments like, 'Why don't you go to bed if you're going to fall asleep on the couch?' Or the most hurtful and recent one: 'Do you really need to talk? I'm watching the game.'" Tears stung my eyes. I hadn't watched another game with him after that. "I was always getting in your way. I got in the way of your law school dreams and obviously your happiness," I raised my voice. "Anyway, good night."

I hung up on him and bawled like a baby, doing my best to stifle my cries so Momma wouldn't hear me. I'd already woken her up too many times the last few months, and tomorrow she had an early shift at the nursing home where she worked as a CNA. Why couldn't I have had a marriage like my parents'? Daddy had thought the sun rose and set with Momma. And as poor as they were, every Monday night he'd come home with one single red rose for her. Each rose stayed in the slender milky-white glass vase in the middle of their tiny kitchen table all week until it was replaced by a new one. It was a reminder of the love Daddy had for Momma. The vase was still there. Since Daddy's untimely death a couple of years ago, I'd made sure Momma had a red rose to fill it each week. I knew it wasn't the same, but I couldn't stand the thought of that vase being empty. I didn't want Momma to feel the emptiness I felt right now, which was paralyzing.

As soon as I got my last shudders out and wiped my eyes, Jake called again. I didn't answer. Nothing was going to change. I needed to face that.

I got back to work, and Jake called again and again and again. Each time I ignored him. He finally texted, which was kind of a big deal for him. He was like a grumpy old man when it came to using technology. "Why can't people just pick up the phone and call? It's much more efficient," he would grumble.

Kasie, I'm sorry. Please answer my call.

It wasn't often he apologized; it was about as rare as him texting.

When he called again, I answered on the third ring, though I didn't say anything.

"Kasie, I'm sorry. Please don't hang up."

I let out a heavy sigh. "Is it really going to matter, Jake?"

"I hope so." He said it quietly, but it was as loud as he had been when it came to trying to salvage our relationship.

"I'm listening." I held in my breath tight, hoping Jake wouldn't disappoint me.

"Kasie, I never meant to hurt you or make you feel like you got in my way. I liked it when we would watch games together."

"No, you didn't."

"I did," he said firmly. "I know I took my frustrations out on you and I shouldn't have. It was never you I was upset with. How could I be, Kasie? You always made do with what we had, and you never complained, even though you had every right to. After all, it's me who got you pregnant. I messed up my own dreams. Not you."

I grabbed my breaking heart. "See, that's the difference between you and me. You and Maribelle were part of my dream. Not the way it happened, of course—but Jake, I always hoped you'd be in my life." The tears were back, streaming down my face. "And just so you know, I also had dreams that didn't come true." My ire was back up. "I wanted to go to the fashion institute. I wanted more babies. I wanted a husband who would kiss me goodbye in the morning and have a hard time stopping because he didn't want to leave me. Then when he came home at night, I wanted him to come right back to my lips because he missed me. But I didn't get any of those things. You're not the only one who didn't get what they wanted."

He remained silent. So silent I thought maybe he'd hung up.

"Jake," I whispered.

"I'm here. I should have been better about kissing you goodbye and hello. But I didn't know you wanted more kids."

"Yes, you did. But every time I brought it up you

would say it wasn't the right time or we couldn't afford it. After a while I figured you didn't want more kids with me, so I never brought it up again." That was ten years ago.

"Damn it, that's not true. I could never pick a better momma for my babies than you. You don't know how awful I felt watching you labor with Maribelle for thirty-six hours while refusing to take anything for the pain for fear you would hurt her. I didn't want to see you hurt like that ever again, especially knowing it was me who placed you in that position. And I always felt guilty for getting you pregnant in the first place."

"If I remember correctly, we were both willing participants during conception."

"Yeah, well, my part was easy, wasn't it?"

"You seemed to enjoy yourself," I teased.

"I always do when we make love."

A surge of heat filled my cheeks. "Really? Sometimes I wondered if . . . well . . . I just wondered is all."

"Kasie," he said tenderly, "I've always felt honored when you've shared your beautiful body with me."

"You think I'm beautiful?" I felt like such a schoolgirl asking him that, but it had been a long time since he'd called me beautiful.

"I don't think. I know."

I bit my lip. "So, what does this mean?"

"I was thinking maybe you wouldn't mind if . . ." he paused and cleared his throat. "What I'm trying to say is, since you used our joint account to pay for swing dance lessons, maybe I should take them with you."

He had rendered me speechless. I had to take a second to make sure I was truly comprehending what he was saying. "You know we'll have to pay extra."

"I figured as much."

"I thought you didn't like girlie things." I couldn't believe this was happening and wanted to give him every out in case he didn't really want to.

"I'm finding I'm missing a lot of girlie things lately."

"Things like me?" I said with all the hope I had in me.

"You're number one on the list."

My face burst into a huge smile. "I miss you too, Jake. Get your dancing shoes ready."

Chapter three

BLESS YOUR HEART. CALL me if you need to talk, honey.

Are you all right?

I hate her for you.

Do you need chocolate? I'm going to Costco to get you the commercial-size bags.

My phone started exploding with random cryptic texts from friends near and far, and from some people I hadn't heard from in forever while I was getting ready for my date with my husband. I was waxing, plucking, teasing, and shining whatever I could. It'd been forever since we'd been on a date, and I couldn't believe he was taking me to a swing dancing class. It meant a lot of up-close-and-personal contact, and I was going to be ready for it. That was, after I figured out why I was being inundated with messages. For a minute I thought maybe people were simultaneously texting the wrong person, but that made no sense whatsoever.

I texted a few people back to see what all the fuss was about before I turned back to the mirror and swiped on pink lip gloss and put on mascara, naively not as worried as I should have been. I was more concerned by the reflection in the tiny bathroom mirror. My green eyes seemed more vibrant and alive than they had been as of late. Even my strawberry blonde hair was having a great day. I'd put it up in a romantic updo and let some curled strands frame my face. It was as if my body was revving up for Jake.

Before I could read any responses, my phone rang.

"Hey, Abs. What's up? I thought you were working tonight."

"I am," her voice shook. "Honey, is your momma with you?"

"Yes." Some worry crept in. "Oh my gosh. Is something wrong with Maribelle?" Is that what all the texts were about?

"No, but . . ."

"Please just spit it out." My heart was racing.

"Go turn on the TV. Channel 4."

"What? Why?"

"You need to see something."

"Please tell me."

"Honey, hurry."

I raced down the hall to the living room. Momma was on the old brown couch that had seen better days, sitting in scrubs with her feet propped up on the coffee table, sipping on a gin martini like she was in a nightclub listening to Sinatra.

I swiped the remote off the arm of the couch and turned it to Channel 4.

"Hey, Patrick Swayze was just going to shove Kelly up against the wall and decimate her lips. I was going to live vicariously through her," Momma

32

complained. She loved *Road House*. She watched it at least once a week. And oddly, when Momma was younger, she had looked quite a bit like Kelly Lynch, who played Dr. Clay in the movie. They both had long blonde hair that had darkened over time, pale-blue eyes, and great cheekbones.

"Sorry." I plopped down next to her, my eyes glued to the screen. Before I knew it, the most annoying women in Nashville popped up, talking in some fancy kitchen that probably no one cooked in. It was way too clean. "Abs," I complained. "Why are you having me watch *Wives of Nashville?*"

"Oh, honey, just wait."

"Wait for—"

"Jake Baldwin is the one who got away," Vivian professed, clutching something to her enhanced chest. I didn't remember her being that well-endowed back in high school. I wasn't sure what was getting lost in the sea of her bosom because I couldn't focus, as my ears were still ringing with my husband's name.

I put Abs on speaker and set my phone on the coffee table.

"Why is she talking about Jake?" Momma and I said at the same time.

"What does she mean, he's the one who got away?" I added in, sick to my stomach.

Abs's silence didn't bode well for me.

My question was answered when they did a flashback scene, and there she was with my husband doing a test drive. That made no sense. For one, Jake didn't work the sales floor anymore—he managed the team. And even if he happened to be on the floor, the sales associates didn't go on the test drives. They let the potential buyers go on their own. But maybe Jake had wanted to get an up-close look at the tiny low-cut sweater Vivian was wearing. It was definitely leaving nothing to the imagination. I mean, even I had the urge to poke the TV screen as if I would be able to tell what those fake babies felt like. There was no denying, though, how stunning Vivian was with her long brunette tresses and pouty red lips. Not to mention her perfectly shaped body that had all the right curves.

I looked down at the flared dress I had made especially for my date tonight. The simple black bodice and black-and-white floral skirt felt almost dowdy in comparison to Vivian's getup.

"Both the driver and passenger seats are heated in this model, as well as the second row," Jake could be heard saying, though the camera was on Vivian.

"Speaking of keeping the seats warm," Vivian purred. "Remember back in high school when you took me to Love Circle? You sure kept me toasty that night." Love Circle was a well-known make out spot in Nashville.

I gasped before throwing my hand over my mouth. I thought I might puke.

Momma slid over on the couch and put her arm around me. "Did you know they dated, baby girl?"

I shook my head. If I spoke, I was going to lose it.

The camera panned over to Jake, who was turning red and rubbing his neck, clearly uncomfortable. "That was a long time ago." He pointed to the dash. "You'll notice that this model comes equipped with an eight-inch high-definition infotainment screen."

"Well, you have me sold," she drawled while reaching over and resting her delicate manicured hand on my husband's thigh. Way too high up.

I jumped up, waiting for my husband to push her hand off and tell her he was married. But the clip ended and suddenly they were in Jake's office. She was signing papers on his desk. "Come sit next to me." She patted the chair next to her. "I need you to explain the fine print here." She pointed at the paper.

Jake reached for the paper across the desk.

She pulled it away. "Come on, silly. I won't bite. After all, we're both married, right? Or is the rumor true? You and your wife are splitting up?" She didn't even try to hide the glee in her voice.

I walked closer to the TV with my hands clenched, waiting for his reply. Internally begging him to tell her he loved me and we were working it out, but his response never came. Instead some dramatic music played before they flashed forward to Vivian and all her cronies. The ladies were dressed like they were going to a club rather than hanging out in a kitchen. They circled Vivian, eagerly waiting for her to speak.

"Y'all, I know I'm married, but being around Jake made me feel things I haven't in so long. He's such a gentleman. And aren't his curls to die for?"

A couple of ladies nodded.

She better keep her hands out of his curls. Before this moment I had never wanted to slap anyone, but I suddenly understood why these ladies had resorted to catfights.

"And those bedroom eyes?" Vivian's voice went all dreamy.

Meanwhile, I couldn't breathe. It was like having a nightmare I couldn't wake up from.

"I know it's sinful," Vivian pretended to be ashamed, "but he told me he and his wife are separated. On the verge of divorce, from the sound of it."

I crumpled and landed on the floor. I thought Jake wanted to work it out.

"What about Beau?" a woman in a slinky silver dress that barely covered her bum asked.

Vivian started to cry. It was obviously fake. "We're drifting apart. I feel like I don't even know him anymore."

One of the ladies patted her shoulder. A few, though, rolled their eyes. I liked those women. Then my stomach dropped when Vivian said, "Look what Jake gave me." She ripped the gift from her bosom.

"Nooo!" Abs screamed.

Momma started swearing, and words were flying out of her mouth so fast it sounded like she was speaking in tongues.

As for me, my eyeballs were glued to the picture of my husband pushing our baby girl on a swing. Tears gushed down my cheeks—grateful at least they had blurred out Maribelle. Regardless, I felt as if I had been stabbed in the heart. I'd given Jake that framed picture several years ago for Father's Day. Why would he give that to her?

Vivian answered my question. "He told me to take this, as a hope for the future. I think he wants to have a baby with me," she squealed like a pig. "And you know, since Beau doesn't have any strong swimmers, I'm considering it." Her violet eyes lit up like the Fourth of July.

Some vomit rose in my throat. I swallowed it back down, leaving a nasty aftertaste in my mouth—just like Jake and Vivian had. "Momma," I cried.

Momma dropped to the ground and held me like a child while I wailed.

"I'll come over tomorrow morning," Abs called out. "I'm so sorry. I love you, girl. Hang in there."

"How could he?" I managed to get out through my sobs.

"I don't know, baby girl. But I'm going to rip him to shreds."

I felt so sucker punched by it all. Jake and I had been talking the last couple of days. Nothing earth shattering, yet we were communicating. You'd think he could have mentioned he was leaving me for Vivian. Or even that he had seen her, for that matter. I would think being on a TV show would be a big deal to him, but maybe he wanted to humiliate me. He'd done a good job.

Above the sound of my sobs, the doorbell rang.

In a panic, I clung to Momma. "I can't see him right now." I couldn't believe he had the audacity to show up. He was a bigger jerk than I ever imagined possible.

"Shh, honey. Don't you worry your beautiful head. Momma is going to take care of him." She left me curled up in a ball on the living room floor's shag carpet and marched toward the door. When she tore it open, a gust of cold air whipped through the room and my heart.

"Hi, Jo, is Kasie ready?" Jake asked, as if nothing had happened.

"You have a lot of nerve coming here tonight after what you just did to my daughter," Momma spewed.

"What are you talking about?" Jake played innocent. That was not the right approach for him to take. I didn't even have to look at Momma to know she was like a boiling pot ready to explode.

"You want me to tell you what I'm talking about? Okay."

I could hear the metaphorical lid pop off.

Jake had better back up or he was going to get burned by the steam he'd just unleashed.

"How dare you go traipsing around with Vivian Jennings behind my girl's back and then have the balls to let a camera crew catch you in the act of fornicating. If I wasn't afraid to hurt my hand, I'd put a knot on your head that not even Oral Roberts would have been able to take off."

When that line came out, you knew she was livid. That used to be one of my nana's favorite sayings.

"What the hell are you talking about? I sold the woman a car last week. End of story."

"Oh, really? Well, you and your girlfriend should get your stories straight before she goes blabbing them all over national TV and showing off the picture you gave her of yourself and my sweet Maribelle."

"Jo." I could hear the frustration in his voice. "Let me talk to my wife."

"Wife," she scoffed. "Don't you call my angel girl your wife. You don't deserve to. You know, Jake, I haven't always agreed with you or even liked the way you treated my daughter at times, but I respected you. I was even proud of the way you took responsibility after Kasie found out she was pregnant. I remember watching you in the delivery room holding Kasie's hand, trying to comfort her, and how in awe you were when they put Maribelle in your arms. I thought, 'He's a good kid.' Even over the years when I would get frustrated that you weren't as attentive to my daughter as I hoped you would be, Billy would say, 'Give the boy some time. He's young and rough around the edges, but he'll come around, don't you worry.' Well, I've been worrying for the last five months. It was bad enough you let her walk out the door. Worse when you didn't come around asking her to come home. But this, Jake," Momma's voice cracked, "this I didn't see coming. You are no longer welcome here." She slammed the door in his face.

Momma rushed to my side. She stroked my hair. "Are you all right, baby girl?"

"No, Momma. My marriage is over."

Chapter Four

AFTER A NIGHT OF blubbering and talking my daughter out of driving back home, I was emotionally and physically exhausted, yet I knew sleep wouldn't come. I went to my room anyway to be alone with my self-deprecating thoughts. Like maybe I should have gotten a boob job, or maybe I should have done more Pilates. I had thought I'd done a good job of keeping my figure, and I'd always tried to do my hair and makeup every day, though I never believed in wearing a lot, unlike a certain tramp who will not be named. It wasn't enough, apparently. I was never enough for Jake.

I think, though, that I felt worse for Maribelle. She'd been trying so hard to stay neutral. She thought of herself as Switzerland, trying to broker a peace deal between her parents. But, tonight, she was all team Momma and ready to declare war on her daddy. Her hero had fallen, and she was devastated. She'd even refused to take his calls. I was ignoring his calls as well. I'd had to turn off my phone because he, and what felt like the entire world, kept calling.

I slowly padded down the hall in the dark, feeling

like I was drunk even though I hadn't had a drop to drink. My head was pounding and I was swaying back and forth, so wiped out. I opened my bedroom door and flipped on the lights. There sat Jake on my bed. I was so startled I let out a tiny yelp and slammed the door behind me.

"Honey, are you okay?" Momma called from the living room. She'd stayed up with me. She had even offered to let me sleep in her room.

Jake jumped up; his eyes were red, and his curls were disheveled. He was dressed nice in a dark pair of jeans and a light blue button-up. He'd obviously put in some effort for our date that had never happened. Or maybe he was dressing up to celebrate the end of us. "Please don't tell your momma I'm here. I need to talk to you."

"We have nothing to say to each other." I slid my wedding ring off and chucked it at his head.

Unfortunately, he had excellent hand-eye coordination and caught it with one hand. He stared down at the ring that looked so tiny in his large hand. "Please," he begged.

I'd never heard him so distraught. "Give me one good reason." I backed up toward the door.

"I love you."

I let out a maniacal laugh. "I don't believe you." I grabbed the doorknob.

"Please, Kasie."

"Kasie, are you okay?" Momma was getting closer to my door.

"Please, Kasie," Jake mouthed while slipping my ring into his pocket.

I closed my eyes and debated. Did I really want blood on my hands? Momma would either kill him or call the cops, and I didn't want to draw any more attention to myself. "I'm fine, Momma. My eyes were playing tricks on me and I thought I saw a rodent." I made sure to look at Jake. He was such a rat.

"Okay, darlin'. I'm across the hall if you need anything. Love you."

"Love you." I locked my door and waited until Momma closed her own and turned her bedroom TV on. She needed the noise to fall asleep. When I felt it was finally safe to speak, I whispered, "How long have you been here?" I looked at the window he always used to sneak into my room during high school. After I moved back home, I kept hoping he would make some grand gesture and sneak into my room and take me in his arms like he used to—love me until I couldn't catch my breath.

I leaned against my dresser for support. I didn't want to think about all those nights when I was stupid enough to believe he loved me.

He stepped closer. "A couple of hours. By the way, I'm going to come back tomorrow and put security locks on the windows. They're too easy to break into."

I rolled my eyes. "Don't act like you care about my well-being. I've been here for five months, Jake, while you've been doing God knows what with Vivian." My eyes filled with tears.

Jake's face turned ten shades of red. "That damn show was all a lie. I saw her once last week when she came in to buy a car. I didn't even want to get involved. I wanted them to use one of my sales guys, but the producers insisted it had to be me. Then Uncle Ray said it was good for business and forced me to do it."

"You never thought to mention this to me?"

"I had to sign some contract and an NDA saying I wouldn't talk about it until it aired. They said it wouldn't be a big deal and I might get thirty seconds of screen time. I honestly didn't think twice about it."

He had gotten a lot more than thirty seconds. I guess they'd liked what they saw. "Right. I mean, why would you say anything? It's not like you gave her a picture of you and our baby. And I saw the way she put her hand on your thigh, and how you looked at her breasts as if you were wondering whether they were light or dark meat and you wouldn't mind a taste."

His jaw dropped. "I don't know how she got that picture. I sure as hell didn't give it to her. And I'm sorry I stared at her chest—it was kind of hard not to. She was practically shoving them in my face. Regardless, do you really think I want to be with a woman like her?"

So perhaps I could give him the breast gawking—even I was fascinated with them. But . . . "I know you do," I spewed. "How many times have we passed her stupid billboards and you've wistfully looked at them as if you're missing out, and then you'll comment about how successful she is? It's like you're saying, 'Kasie, why can't you be more like her?' or 'If only Vivian would have gone to homecoming with me.' Or maybe you were thinking that you should have taken Vivian to Love Circle more often. For all I know, you have been for the last several months. I didn't even know you two had ever dated," I cried.

He tried to wrap his arms around me, but I wasn't having it. I batted him away. "Don't touch me."

He forcefully shoved his hands into his jeans pockets. "We went out a couple of times in high school before you and I started dating. I didn't think I needed to mention it. I never asked you who you dated before me. Why should it matter?"

"Did you sleep with her?" I pleaded to know. My entire body clenched waiting for him to respond.

He let out a heavy breath. "How can you ask me that? You know very well you were the first girl I made love to. I fumbled through everything our first time together. Don't you remember? I had no idea what the hell I was doing."

All I remembered was how sweet he was about it. How he'd kept asking if he was hurting me or if I was okay. He must have said he loved me a hundred times that night. That was all in the past, though. "Well, you know what you're doing now. Has she been benefiting from your experience?"

His wide eyes made it look like I had slapped him. "Kasie," he said, low. "I've done a lot of things I'm not proud of, but one thing I'm not is a cheater. You are the only woman I have ever made love to."

I didn't know whether I could believe him or not. "You humiliated me and our baby tonight." Tears trickled down my cheeks. "Do you have any idea what it's like to have the person you love most in the world publicly announce they don't want you?"

"Damn it, Kasie, I didn't do that. They manipulated everything. But while we're on the subject, yes, I have an inkling what it's like to have my wife leave me and for everyone to know about it," he spat.

"You said you didn't love me, Jake. What did you want me to do?"

He ran his hands through his hair. "I never said that."

"Yeah, well, you didn't disagree with me."

He sat back down on my bed and scrubbed a hand over his face. "I know," he whispered. "I'm sorry, Kasie. I've been regretting it every day." He blew out a large breath. "Every night I come home to my own special hell—the one I created. Each time I walk into our room, I expect to see you with your hair splayed all over the pillow, lying there in one of my T-shirts, waiting to be loved. But all I see is an empty bed. I tell myself to quit being a stubborn bastard and beg you to come home. To tell you I love you. Then the following morning my pride gets the better of me, and I go on living in hell."

"You don't love me," I choked out. "I don't think you ever did. I'm the 'love the one you're with' woman."

He narrowed his eyes. "What does that even mean?"

"Like the song says—if you can't be with the one you love, love the one you're with. You didn't get to be with Vivian. And if I hadn't gotten pregnant, you wouldn't have stayed with me either."

His jaw clenched. "Have you always felt this way?"

"For a long time." I shuddered.

He hung his head. "I've been a worse husband than I thought."

I slid down against the dresser and sat on the floor, so exhausted.

"If that's how you truly feel, I don't blame you for not believing me about Vivian. But Kasie, with God as my witness, I don't want to be with that woman. She's a psycho. Sure, I've been envious of her success, but I never wanted you to be like her. And I could have had her a dozen times back in high school after you and I started dating. She made herself plenty available to me. But why would I when I had the prettiest, sweetest girl in the world?"

My lips quivered and a huge ball of emotion got caught in my throat. "A long time ago when you used to say that, I believed you. But for the last few years, I've felt like I don't even exist to you."

He looked up to the ceiling. "What your momma said tonight cut to the bone. I know I haven't treated you like you deserve. I've been unhappy with life, and I took it out on you."

"Why are you so unhappy?"

He lowered his head and his electric blue eyes hit me. "Because I wanted more. I felt like I missed out."

"I wasn't enough," I eeked out.

"Kasie," he choked up, "these last few months made me realize you were everything. I've had all this time to do whatever I want, and the only thing I want is you."

I rubbed my chest where my heart beat out of control, wishing so much that he was telling the truth.

How could I believe him, though? "You didn't come for me."

"No, I didn't," he said with deep regret. "Tonight, I had every intention of asking you to come home, but after talking to you, I realize I don't deserve you. I'm sorry for what I did to make you believe I wanted you to be anyone other than who you are. Vivian was never your competition. I was, and I hate myself for it." He stood and looked down at me so tenderly. "I'm going to go now. I love you, Kasie. I have from the moment I first held you in my arms. I should have done a better job of holding on. But now you deserve for me to let go."

I blinked and blinked, stunned and confused. I didn't know whether I could believe him or not, but . . . "That's it? We're over?" Just like that even though we had been together for over half my life.

"It's for the best," his voice hitched.

"Is it?" All of a sudden, I wasn't so sure.

Jake knelt next to me. With tears rolling down his cheeks, he ran the back of his hand down my cheek. I'd never seen him cry like this before.

"I'm never going to hurt you again," he promised. He leaned in and barely brushed his lips across mine.

My lips screamed out that they wanted more, while my head said it wasn't so sure and that maybe Jake leaving was for the best. The thought made my heart shatter into a million pieces. "Jake," I choked out.

"I know, Kasie. It's not what I wanted for us either, but you deserve a better man." He stood so fast it was like if he didn't, he would change his mind. He stared around my cramped room filled with shipping supplies and fabric. "You should come home. The house is yours. I'll go stay with Dallas."

"I don't think I could live there without you." I didn't know how I was going to live without him, period.

"Please," he begged. "That house is the only thing I ever did right by you."

"Jake, that's not true."

"Name one other thing." He sounded desperate.

"You've always been a good daddy."

His brow furrowed in consternation. "Tell me something I did for you." He was issuing it like a challenge he knew couldn't be met.

I wanted to reach out to him, to comfort him, but my hands stayed put in my lap, so torn about who, what, or how to believe. I'd never seen him so downtrodden, and in that moment, I ached to make him feel better. "Jake, I can name at least a hundred things, but I always think about how good you were to me when I was trying to learn how to cook. You ate every awful thing I ever made and never complained. You even had seconds when I knew darn well the food wasn't fit for a dog. But you swallowed it down and thanked me just the same."

Jake flashed me a crooked grin. "Well, you turned into a good cook. Real good." He patted his flat stomach. He'd definitely lost some weight in the last few months.

"Are you eating okay?" I couldn't help but ask.

"I get by. I'm good at microwaving TV dinners. The salsa you canned last summer makes about anything taste good." He cleared his throat. "I should probably get going. Bye, Kasie Ann," he said with such emotion it made my eyes water. "I do love you." He turned and headed for the window before I could respond.

"You can go out the front door," I said, not knowing what else to say. I was so confused. Visions of that stupid TV show kept going through my head, mixed in with the broken man I saw in front of me. Where did the truth lie?

"I don't want to wake up your momma. I know she sleeps with a shotgun under the bed."

"That's probably a good call." A tiny laugh escaped. Though none of this was funny at all. "Bye, Jake," I whispered, my soul dying as I breathed out those words.

He was silent as he climbed out the window into the dark and cold. It was exactly how I felt. It was so all-encompassing I wondered if I would ever feel light and warmth again. Though these last five months hadn't been easy, I'd at least had hope. Tonight, every bit of it had faded away, and I longed for it and the man I loved. I looked down at my empty ring finger and sobbed. How had it all gone so wrong?

Chapter Five

"POOKIE BEAR, WHY DO I keep getting so many comments on Instagram asking me if I have hair extensions?" Vivian whined to her husband while looking at her reflection in her cell phone. "I mean, look at me. Do I look like I would use someone else's hair or fake polyester extensions?"

Pookie bear, I mean Beau, took another long drink of bourbon then slammed the glass on their kitchen counter before walking out of the room.

"What's wrong with him?" Vivian asked herself.

"Oh, I don't know," I snarled at the screen. "Maybe it's that you're keeping a picture of my husband on your nightstand, you psycho."

"Sugar, maybe we should turn the TV off." Abs grabbed my hand before it could dive back into the chocolate chip ice cream carton. That's right, I wasn't using a spoon. I could shovel it in faster using my fingers.

"No way. I have to see what happens. Better to get the news firsthand than by phone or at the grocery store. I can't go anywhere anymore without people staring at me. And they haven't even said my name on the stupid show. Yet everyone knows I'm Jake's wife . . . or at least I am for now," I blubbered.

"I think we've had enough sugar for today." Abs grabbed the carton and set it on the coffee table.

"Are you saying I'm getting fat?" I looked down at my T-shirt, which was stained with chocolate. I might have eaten hot fudge like soup earlier.

"Now you're just talking silly. If anyone thinks you're fat, they need to get their eyes checked. But you probably could do with some protein today or maybe a vegetable."

I leaned against her and groaned.

She wrapped an arm around me. "Have you talked to Jake?"

"Not since I moved back in last week and he moved out. Even then we hardly spoke. He just kissed my cheek and said goodbye," I croaked.

"So, you believe Vivian's version about what happened?"

"I don't know," I moaned. "I mean, she's not letting it drop. Why is she keeping his picture and talking about him all the time?" Like right now. I focused back on the screen. Vivian was with all the other wives getting mani-pedis. Because what else do you have to do in the middle of the day with half a dozen women? Other than take pole dancing lessons. They'd done that earlier in the show tonight. That was quite the sight. I was just going to say that maybe Vivian was stripping on the side. She was way too good. Maybe I should have learned how to pole dance. Though I'm pretty sure if I tried, I would break something. Regardless, I thought these women all had high-powered jobs, yet they never seemed to be at work.

"What's up with you and Jake?" Marla taunted Vivian. Marla was my favorite. She didn't take any crap from Vivian, and I was hoping she would slap her.

Vivian sat up straight in her chair while an attractive Latin guy rubbed her legs with a salt scrub. I wasn't sure where this nail salon was located, but the nail techs looked more like bodybuilders and were mostly male.

"Beau doesn't like me to talk about him," she sighed like she was so put-upon.

"Can you blame the guy? You put a picture of Jake in your bedroom." Marla gave her an *Are you dense?* look.

"I just can't stop thinking about him. But," she pouted, "Jake's such a good guy, and he doesn't want to hurt his family, so we're putting the brakes on our relationship. Apparently, his wife wants another chance."

I bolted up. "What! Can I sue them for libel, or slander, or for just being plain stupid and self-absorbed? How does she have any idea what I want? If they can't use my name without my permission, how is it that they can still talk about me?"

I'd received a million emails and phone calls from the producers of the slimy show asking me to come on and give my take. They also wanted permission to use my yearbook photo. The answer was not only no, but heck to the freaking no.

"I'm sure you could," Abs said, "but I guarantee

they are lawyered up. And even if you won, you'd lose more money than it's worth."

"It's so unfair. Meanwhile, I have people stopping me in public trying to offer comfort by giving me tips on how to poison my husband and make it look like an accident."

"Ooh, did you write that down? I wouldn't mind using that on my ex-husband—who, once again, didn't pay alimony this month. I'm still the beneficiary on his life insurance policy."

"Ugh. I'm sorry. Good news, though: orders are up due to everyone feeling sorry for me, so I can pay you more this month. Someone even wanted to start a GoFundMe account to help pay for my divorce expenses."

"Did you let them?"

"No," I whispered. "I don't want to take people's money, and I especially don't want any more drama right now. Maribelle is beside herself already. She doesn't know who or what to believe. Though she's leaning toward believing her daddy. She idolizes the man. I want to believe Jake, but even if he's telling the truth, it's not like our marriage was solid before all this mess." I reached for the ice cream. I was going to eat my feelings into oblivion.

Abs swiped the carton before I could grab it and walked it back to the kitchen. "You'll thank me later."

I held my bloated stomach and fell sideways on the couch. "Probably," I groaned. "What do I do?"

"Sugar," she called from the kitchen. "I'm probably not the best person to ask. I'm pretty anti-husband right now. That said, I was never this torn up when I found out Jimmy was cheating on me. Honestly, it was a relief."

"That telephoto lens was a good purchase." I snickered.

"Best money ever spent. And those black jumpsuits you made for our James Bond spy days were the best."

Abs and I had followed her ex around for a week trying to catch him in the act. We'd hidden in bushes, army crawled, and climbed on strangers' roofs. We were ready for MI6. We only needed the British accents and a weapon more advanced than a camera and some pepper spray.

"Maybe I could market them. Tagline: Is your man a slut? Are you ready to give him the boot? Try our jumpsuit."

Abs roared while walking back into the family room. "You know, I think you might be onto something."

"I'd say we should put them on and spy on Jake, except Dallas says he's home alone every night." He also said Jake was depressed and feeling pretty beat up. Part of me wanted to say that it served him right, but there was a piece of my heart that wanted him to be the man he'd promised me he would be when we got married—faithful and devoted.

Abs took her place back on the couch. "Maybe we still should. I wouldn't mind getting a peek at Dallas in his natural habitat."

I sat up. "Gross. He's like a brother to me. I thought you were anti-men, anyway."

"Anti-husband. There's a difference."

"You know Dallas isn't ever going to settle down."

"I know, which is why I'd never be serious about him. Still, I wouldn't mind letting him mix my grits a time or two, if you get my meaning."

"Unfortunately, I do." I giggled. Not to say I cared how or when people ate their grits. To each his own. In fact, I missed grits. A lot.

"Oh, that Vivian is such a #####!" Marla was bleeped out, but we all knew what she'd called her. It was enough to catch Abs's and my attention. Marla was raging to her husband after the mani-pedis. "She's giving us a bad name."

"Uh, I think the excessive lifestyle and catfights probably aren't helping," Abs interjected.

"Everyone thinks we're a bunch of home-wreckers now. I think she's lying and only doing it to get more time on the show. If only I could prove it and show everyone she's not the victimized angel she wants us all to believe she is."

Cue dramatic music. It was like a bad soap opera.

Marla's husband, who owned a large estate and bred world-class racehorses, looked up from his iPad. "Darlin', prove her wrong, then. I believe in you."

Cue more dramatic music. Enough with the music already. There was no theme music in real life. Although, were these women living a real life?

Marla tapped her finger against her pouty lips. I think having pouty lips was a requirement to get on the show. Or maybe I'd missed an episode where they had all gone to the plastic surgeon together to get collagen injections. You know what they say: friends who inject their lips together, stay together.

"Well, Big D . . ." That's what Marla called her husband. I think it was short for Big Daddy, which, I'm not going to lie, creeped me out a bit considering Big D was twenty-five years older than Marla. But who was I to judge? If she could prove Vivian was a liar, I'd let her call me Mommy.

"I think I have a plan," Marla continued.

They ended the scene there. In a flash, Vivian was back on the screen and she was being shown the clip of Marla calling her out. Vivian started crying—like big fat fake tears. "Why would she think that?" They let her cry for an entire minute of airtime, and then, amazingly, her tears ceased. "I guess we'll see who the angel really is," she sang, very non-angelically. It was enough to send some shivers down my spine.

They ended the show there.

"What?" I protested. "What's Marla's plan?" I yelled at the TV.

"I guess we'll find out next week." Abs shrugged.

They didn't do previews until the day before the next episode aired because, unlike some other reality TV shows, they tried to keep this one as close to real time as possible. They claimed it was the most true-to-life of all reality shows. What a bunch of garbage.

"Ugh," I groaned, hating myself for getting sucked into their world.

Abs patted my leg. "Question is, what if Marla proves Vivian is a liar? Where does that leave you and Jake?"

I looked around our beautiful home, especially at the fire that burned low in our stone fireplace with its deep wood mantel that was filled with family pictures.

Jake was even smiling in a few, though smiling wasn't really his thing. I thought about how proud Jake was of this house. "Abs," I whispered. "For so long, all I wanted was for Jake to love me. Now he says he does and always has, but what if it doesn't last? What if he decides later on down the road that he really missed out? Or what if he only said it because he feels guilty about what happened between him and Vivian?"

"You yourself said Vivian was manipulative and a liar."

"True, but this is a pretty big lie for her to tell, especially so publicly and when she has a husband. I mean, what would be her motivation if it weren't true, or at least partially true?"

Abs blew out a breath that made her bangs take flight. "I don't know, honey. That's a good question. It'll probably be one you never get an answer to. Unless Marla really does have a plan. Most likely, though, it's going to come down to whether you trust Jake or not, and if you're willing to give him another chance. That's the reality of the situation."

"Sometimes reality sucks."

"Amen, sister. Amen."

Chapter Six

I RUBBED MY TIRED eyes that refused to close. When they did, all I saw were visions of Vivian's hand on my husband's thigh; or worse, the way Jake had looked at me, begging me to believe him. His "I love you's" echoed in my head. Why couldn't he have told me earlier how he felt? Or enjoyed the ride we were on together? I was far from perfect, but I'd tried to be a good wife. I'd even tried to understand him, to the point of making too many excuses for his sometimes-distant behavior. I was tired of that. I needed him to be present and love me regardless of what he had given up. Like me, I'd hoped he would see it as a trade-up instead of a trade-off.

I stared at the cute heart-patterned Valentine's Day scrunchies I was making in the middle of the night. Might as well be doing something productive. I took a sip of my dirty Diet Coke for a boost of energy. Before I began cutting more elastic an email notification popped up on my phone. Normally, I would have ignored it, but the sender's address caught my attention: vivianisthedevil@gmail.com. That was my kind of address.

I clicked on my email app and contemplated opening the message. It was a pretty spammy-sounding email address, but what the heck, I thought. A little email virus was nothing compared to what I had been through lately. I clicked on the email.

Dear Kasie,

I'm sending you this video at great risk. I'm going to trust that you won't share it with any media outlets. I thought you should know the truth about what really happened between your husband and Vivian. Don't let her destroy your life like she has mine.

X

Who was X? They sounded as ominous as finding out the truth would be. The truth was sometimes worse than my imagination, and I had imagined a lot of things this past week and over the last several years. I'd wondered if Jake would cheat on me or if he was already. I knew he was unhappy. And I know how some men think—*If I'm not happy in my wife's arms, I will be in another's.*

My thumb hovered over the video link while I swallowed hard. I really wished Abs were here to hold my hand for this. I could be brave, though. I was a mother, after all. No braver job in the world. I squinted my eyes, clicked, and prayed.

My phone screen lit up with what looked like raw, unedited footage of Jake and Vivian on the test drive.

Vivian was having a hard time keeping her eyes on the road. She kept glancing at Jake, who was gripping his seat, looking afraid for his life.

"I heard you and Kasie were separated." Vivian used her *Oh, you poor thing* voice.

"That's none of anyone's business," Jake set her straight.

"Oh, well, I didn't mean to pry," she turned on the charm. "I just wanted to say how sorry I am."

Right. I wanted to shake her.

Jake didn't respond other than to mention that the SUV had a V-8 engine.

Vivian batted her luxurious eyelashes. "You know, you used to rev my engine. Vroom vroom," she giggled.

I wanted to gag.

"I'm married, Vivian." Jake pulled no punches. It made my eyes water. I had a feeling I was going to find out that I, along with all of Tennessee, had falsely accused my husband.

"Not for long, from what I hear." She got braver.

Jake glowered at her. "Who said that?"

"Just a little birdie," she sang.

Jake's pinched face said he wanted to shoot that bird.

There was a break in the footage. The next scene was where that she-devil placed her hand on my husband's thigh. I gripped my worktable, hardly able to watch it. I still felt so ill about it. But a second after her hand landed, Jake pushed it away. "Vivian, I'm married." He seemed to have to remind her of that fact frequently.

"So am I. What of it?" she purred. "Doesn't mean we can't have a little fun. I promise it will be worth your while. You'll have more business and pleasure than you'll know what to do with."

Oh. My. Gosh. Somebody really needed to slap her.

"The only person I'm doing anything with is my wife."

"Aww, Jake," I whispered.

You would have thought that would deter Vivian, but I recognized that look in her eye. Jake had become a challenge. "A lot can happen when people are separated."

Jake glared at her. "I love my wife. Period."

Those words made my heart flutter like the first time he'd said them to me on Christmas day our senior year in high school. I wanted to see the wench's response to Jake's declaration, but the video cut out. The next clip was of her alone in Jake's office while he left to get the keys to her new car. I had to say, I found it fishy that she was even buying a car from Jake. She struck me as someone who drove fancy foreign cars, not a Suburban.

"What are you doing?" someone off camera asked her as she perused the credenza filled with our family pictures and sales awards Jake had won over the years.

"I'm going to make ratings gold." She picked up the picture of Jake and Maribelle. "This one should do the trick." She held up the picture. "She looks like she could be mine, doesn't she?"

My baby looked nothing like her. I was so furious I could feel my blood boil.

"If you say so," the elusive person off camera said.

"I do." Vivian shoved the picture in her Louis Vuitton bag.

The video was over. I sat back, stunned and ashamed. Poor Jake was being accused of awful things online and in the media, even to his face. I myself had been one of his accusers. I couldn't believe Vivian and the producers of that show could get away with this. Something had to be done. The truth had to be known.

I emailed back.

Dear X,

The world needs to know the truth. I'm ready to fight. What can I do?

Kasie

P.S. I want that picture back. Can you help?

I leaned back in my chair, wondering if Jake was up. I wanted to call him and apologize. But how do you apologize for accusing your husband of infidelity? Maybe the better question was, how does your marriage get to the point where you no longer believe your husband? My eyes stung with tears. I knew the answer to that one. It took years of feeling like maybe Jake thought I'd trapped him, even though he was always the first one to shut people down if they suggested such a thing. He'd even raked his parents over the coals for it, to the point that they'd hardly said two words to us after we got married until Maribelle was born. It was amazing what having someone's grandchild could do for their attitude. Not that Pam and Rich were the best in-laws, but Jake had made sure they treated me with respect. And they adored Maribelle. Regardless, sometimes Jake had felt so distant over the last couple of years. It had allowed doubts to creep in.

So maybe the most important question was, did this revelation change anything? If Jake loved me like he said he did, should we really give up?

While I was contemplating, I received another message.

Kasie,

You have me thinking. Perhaps we can kill two birds with one stone. We can prove Vivian to be the liar she is and get your picture back. I have two questions for you. How brave are you, and can you pick a bedroom door lock?

X

I had a feeling I knew where this was going. Good thing I could easily answer those questions.

I had a baby when I was eighteen and was in labor for over thirty-six hours with no pain medication. The girl came out as headstrong as a Category 5 hurricane. Believe me, Vivian is no match. And my best friend has some lock-picking skills.

X's reply was simple.

This is excellent news. Be ready.

Oh, I was ready.

Chapter Seven

"YOU PUNCHED IN THE wrong code," I whispered, a bit on edge. I mean, it wasn't like I was getting ready to sneak into the home of one of the most recognizable women in the country right now. Okay, that was exactly what I was doing.

"Don't get your panties in a wad, darlin'." Dallas tried the code again to get into Vivian's gated community. He had the fanciest car of anyone I knew—a Range Rover. And he was more than willing to help in the heist. Not only was he a troublemaker, but he was willing to do anything in the hope that Jake would move out of his place. I'd warned Dallas this was no guarantee that Jake and I were getting back together. In fact, I hadn't even told Jake about the video yet. I thought maybe I should get the picture back first and then we should talk face-to-face.

"Don't fuss at him," Abs scolded me. "You'll only make him nervous."

I rolled my eyes. She was sitting in the front with Dallas, and the two had been flirting nonstop on the drive over here.

Dallas flashed Abs a devilish grin. "I'm excellent under pressure," he drawled.

Even in the dark, I could see Abs blush. "Is that so? Would you like to prove that to me?"

Oh. My. Hello Kitty. I'd started saying that instead of *hell* when Maribelle was younger because there was nothing like your six-year-old telling your pastor that he gave a hell of a sermon. "Y'all, we are kind of in the middle of something important here. Can we push pause on the flirtation button?"

"I like the sound of pushing buttons," Dallas said seductively. "Just tell me where."

Abs giggled.

I threw up my hands and fell back against the seat. "I can't deal with you two."

Dallas turned around and pursed his lips together. "Now, darlin', don't go acting like someone licked the red off your candy. I got this under control." Without looking, he reached out of the car window and punched in the code X had given me. The large wrought iron gate began to swing in, allowing us access to one of the glitziest neighborhoods in Nashville—Forest Hills.

"See, darlin', I got this."

I blew out a deep breath. I was glad someone had this under control. I didn't know why I was doing this. If I wanted to, I could have had the picture reprinted and bought a new frame for Jake. It was just that something about Vivian got under my skin. The way she and the show's producers manipulated those videos was wrong. They were intentionally hurting people's lives. The lives I cared most about in the

65

world—Maribelle's and Jake's. Even if Jake could be insensitive, I still loved the man. He was my first love, my only love.

I swallowed my nerves back down as we crept past a few well-lit mansions on the way toward Vivian's. I kept running the plan over in my mind. X had said that Vivian was holding a charity event at her house for a local hospital. X said she was only doing it to come off as a saint to the community, but all the wives had to attend. X assured me we could slip in through the nanny quarters undetected and make our way to the master bedroom. I wasn't sure why people with no children had nanny quarters. I was also curious as to why X had called Vivian's master bedroom *the lair* and why Vivian was apparently hyper-particular that it always remained locked. The way X told it, Vivian herself had taken the footage they'd used of the picture on her nightstand. Sounded suspicious to me.

I had asked X if she was one of the wives, but his/her only response was that it was neither here nor there. All that mattered was putting Vivian in her place. I admit, I probably liked the sound of that too much and would need to visit my pastor after this was all said and done. There was some major repenting on the horizon. Hopefully, though, no one would be the wiser that I was basically breaking and entering. Technically, only entering. X promised the nanny quarters would be unlocked. So maybe Abs would be breaking in when she worked her magic on the bedroom door lock. But we were only going in to get back what had been stolen from me in the first place.

In exchange for X's help getting the picture back,

I'd promised I would post on my social media pages that the picture was back in my possession and that I knew Jake had been faithful to me. I hoped it would put to rest all the negative things being said about Jake and shut Vivian up.

It was all going to be a piece of cake. I hoped.

Dallas parked on a little side road that looked like it was used for whoever maintained the grounds in the prestigious neighborhood. It gave us a decent view of Vivian's grand white home with its columns worthy of the Parthenon, especially since I came equipped with binoculars—another purchase Abs and I had made when we were spying on her lousy ex-husband. We were also wearing our black jumpsuits. Who knew how much use we would get out of our spy gear?

While I scoped out the place, Dallas and Abs continued with their antics. Not sure what had gotten into them, they had never been so flirty before. Maybe the adrenaline rush of knowing we were doing something a little dangerous had gotten their blood going. Or perhaps it was the black jumpsuit. Abs had some serious curves and the jumpsuit brought them all out.

I tried ignoring them as I watched people walk in, but when Abs said, "A girl needs to know, how do you like your grits: sweet or savory?" I had no choice but to pay attention.

"Darlin', this boy goes both ways."

"Excuse me, I'm in the car, and I don't need to feel any queasier than I already do. Would y'all like me to give you a moment?"

"Would you mind?" Dallas teased—maybe.

Abs laughed. "Sorry, sugar. What do you see?"

JENNIFER PEEL

It took a second to get the image of them mixing grits together out of my head. "Um . . . do you see the line of pine trees there?" I pointed. "I think we can use those for cover until we get to the side of the house where the nanny entrance should be." I pulled out the crudely drawn map of the house X had sent me.

Dallas took it out of my hands and examined it. "Are you sure this X person is trustworthy?"

I tossed my head from side to side. "I think so?" I said, not 100 percent sure.

Dallas chuckled. "You either have a few screws loose or you're in love with my brother."

"Both," I whispered.

Dallas ruffled my hair, which was pulled up in a spy bun. "You and Jake are both a mess. I don't think he could find his butt right now even if he stuck his hands in his back pockets. Don't know why either one of you thought you could be without the other."

"We weren't doing all that great together."

"That may be, but I've never seen a love like the two of you have. You fought hard to be together and stay together even though the odds were against you. That ought to say something."

"I don't know, Dallas," I sighed.

"Girl, you're about ready to storm a castle—what does that say to you?"

"That I've lost my ever-loving mind."

"Agreed. Just make sure you get the job done. I'm tired of hearing Jake moan and whine every night about how much he misses you."

I bit my lip. "He does?"

68

"What do you think he's doing? Baking cupcakes?"

"I don't know, but I can't think about it right now. I'm about to commit larceny. Sort of."

"Won't be the first time," Abs sang.

We both smiled thinking about the time we'd broken into her ex Jimmy's truck. He'd taken her wedding ring to pawn it after she'd kicked him out. The idiot should have gone straight to the pawnshop, but he'd stopped off for a few beers at the bar. Let's just say I'm pretty good with a coat hanger. And we went and pawned that baby ourselves.

"We were only taking back what was rightfully yours," I reminded her.

"That's all we're doing tonight too." She tapped my nose. "We should probably get going. We've been through the plan plenty."

That was true—we'd been talking nonstop about it for the last few days.

"Keep your phone on," I implored Dallas. "I'll text you as soon as we're on our way out. Make sure the car is running so we can get the Hello Kitty out of Dodge."

"Breathe," Dallas laughed. "This isn't my first rodeo either."

I didn't even want to know what kind of rodeos he'd been to.

"Okay," I exhaled loudly. "Let's do this."

Dallas grabbed Abs's jumpsuit with no warning and pulled her close. "A kiss for good luck." He laid one on her.

Abs was rendered starstruck and practically

melted into her seat. I literally watched her arms go limp.

Those Baldwin boys knew how to kiss you until your toes curled and both your ovaries popped out eggs begging for the chance to become their offspring.

"Hey, knock it off," I complained. "She's going to be useless to me if you keep going, and I might vomit." More like turn green with envy. I missed Jake's kisses like a baby missed milk.

Dallas put his finger to my mouth, shushing me, while still gripping my best friend. When she gasped, I hopped out of the car into the cold night. If they started mixing grits, I was calling for backup. Jake knew how to pick locks. He'd broken into my house plenty of times when we were growing up. Hence the reason I was in this situation. Not to say I would change our past. I wouldn't. As stupid as we'd been, I cherished those early days and many days since.

I wondered what Jake would think about me doing all this. He'd probably say to let it be. Except that was the problem with our marriage. We'd let too many things be instead of facing them head-on. Like when we had found out we were going to have a baby. Jake had put up a brave front. He'd told me we would beat the odds. We had been so naïve—we'd thought Jake could still go to school and I could work with a baby. Then Maribelle came and we found out that babies needed constant attention and daycare was too expensive. We'd never dealt with Jake's disappointment; we had pushed it aside, just trying to make ends meet and survive on little to no sleep.

Or whenever I had expressed my worries that

things weren't right in our marriage, Jake would typically put a Band-Aid on them in the form of sending me flowers or taking me to dinner. Sex was usually involved. But nothing ever really changed. Then I walked away, and he let me. That hurt more than anything. But regardless of what ended up happening in our marriage, I wasn't going to let Vivian spread lies about us.

I rubbed my arms from the cold and readied myself to storm the castle, as Dallas put it. I peeked over my shoulder to see Abs and Dallas were still going at it. Oh, my Hello Kitty. We were in the middle of an operation. I knocked on the window, and they broke apart.

I rolled my eyes at their disheveled state. "I'm going in without you if I have to," I called through the closed, slightly fogged up window. Man, I needed a good make out session.

Abs righted herself while smiling like a cat who had caught a big fat mouse. I hoped Dallas wouldn't break her heart. I was beginning to think there was no recovery after a Baldwin boy got to you. I knew Abs said she wouldn't take him seriously, but a Baldwin boy could get under your skin and touch every part of your soul before you even knew what hit you.

I decided to start walking toward Vivian's in the hope that Abs would start following along. We didn't have all night and there was a lull in cars arriving. Hopefully, that meant everyone coming to the party was already there. Thankfully, Abs took the hint, and before I knew it she was next to me, swaying from side to side like she was drunk. I knew that feeling. Jake could make my head spin. I steadied her and laughed.

"Whoa." She breathed out and pulled her hair back up into a ponytail.

"I warned you."

"Sugar, I just had a life-changing experience. Praise Jesus." She held her hands up to the sky.

"Thanks for letting me be a witness." My tone oozed sarcasm.

She giggled. "Sorry, honey, but I have no regrets. Momma needed that."

I linked arms with her. "Believe me, I get it. Please, though, for the love of everything good and holy, wait until I'm out of the car next time."

"Deal. You ready for this?"

I stared at the mansion looming in front of us and let out a deep breath. "Ready or not, here we go."

Chapter Eight

WE HID BEHIND A large pine tree, staring at the security camera above the nanny entrance.

"Are you sure this X said they would take care of the camera situation?" Abs whispered.

"They promised," I eeked out, wondering if maybe we should turn back. But my pride kept my feet firmly planted. Visions of Vivian touching Jake and her taunting me during high school fed the proud monster, while whispers of Jake telling Vivian that he loved me filled me with righteous indignation. I was tired of Jake's name being dragged through the mud. He'd never let anyone disparage me, and I owed it to him to set the record straight.

"Why couldn't this X person just give you the picture?"

"Something about how they didn't want to start a holy war and they would be the first suspect."

"I bet Marla is X," Abs surmised.

Marla was my first guess too. Maybe this was the plan she'd mentioned on the last show and I was a pawn on her chessboard.

"Do you want to turn back?" I asked Abs, kind of hoping she would be the voice of reason and beat the Hello Kitty out of my pride.

"No way, sugar. This is the most fun I've had in a long time."

I wasn't sure I would say it was fun now that we were here. Sure, the idea had sounded good at the time, but now that reality was slapping me, I wasn't so convinced.

Abs, sensing my hesitation, took the lead and made sure the coast was clear before grabbing my hand and sashaying toward the nanny door like we owned the place. My heart was pumping when we made it to the door, not from exertion but from adrenaline kicking in. I let out a whoosh and my breath danced in the cold air. I rubbed my hands, red from the chilly temp, while saying a prayer before I tried the door. Not sure God was really into answering prayers regarding pseudo crimes; regardless, I reminded him that Vivian had started it by stealing the picture and that she wanted to commit adultery. I figured I was doing my part in preventing a serious sin from occurring, so God should be thankful for my willingness to break and enter.

Whether he was or not, no alarms went off when I turned the knob and opened the door. Praise.

Both Abs and I took a moment to lean on the closed door once we were inside. We held hands like our lives depended on it.

"We're in," I whispered.

Abs nodded and breathed a sigh of relief.

The room was dark, yet we could see the outline

of furniture and what looked like a kitchenette. I wondered why they had furniture for a nonexistent nanny. Heaven forbid Vivian procreated. We didn't need any more of her crazy genes in the human pool.

Above us there was a lot of noise. People were talking and the music was thumping. This was good— more cover for us.

I pointed to a door across the way. "The map says that door leads to a set of stairs that will take us to the master bedroom wing. How pretentious is that?" I rolled my eyes.

"Sugar, you know what they say: pretentious people are like a cross-stitch piece—pretty in the front and a big ole mess in the back."

I had to stifle my giggle. "I believe there is some truth there. All right, let's do this."

Abs and I held hands as we tiptoed across the dark room. When we passed the couch in the living area, Abs pointed at the blanket, pillows, and bottle of bourbon on the coffee table. "I would say this is where Beau has been sleeping."

Crap. "Let's hope he doesn't make it an early night."

"Are you kidding me? He has to keep up appearances for the camera crew they have upstairs."

"Don't remind me. If we get caught, I don't want this recorded."

"It'll be fine, sugar," Abs tried to reassure me.

I nodded, praying God was on our side. I would even take Lady Luck at this point.

We made it to the next door without incident and, thankfully, it was unlocked. When we opened the door, a darkened staircase greeted us. Without saying a word, we both turned on our cell phone flashlights like we were pros. We took each step up the wooden stairs as if they were going to be our last. I felt like we were in a haunted house and something was going to pop out and chop off my head. Thankfully, this wasn't our first "crime" and we had both worn soft-soled shoes.

When we reached the top of the spiral staircase, we paused. It felt as though each door we'd reached was the next level of Jumanji, and I was sure a rush of rhinos was going to come barreling through this one. So far, everything had gone according to plan and X had been good to his/her word. With all that I was, I hoped it stayed that way.

"There's no turning back once we go through this door," I squeaked.

Abs smiled. "Sugar, was there ever a question of us retreating?"

I smiled back. "Probably not. I'm too stubborn."

She squeezed my hand. "Let's go save your relationship."

I leaned back. "What?"

"Oh, honey, don't play dumb with me. I saw the tears in your eyes when you showed me that video. Not to mention, I heard the longing in Jake's voice. I'm not going to lie—I'm jealous. No man ever said he loved me the way Jake said he loved you. Don't tell me you didn't feel that in your bones."

I wiped the corner of my eye with my free hand. "Abs, I'm scared. I believe Jake loves me and the good Lord knows I've been head over heels for him since the day I laid eyes on him. But I need more than words. I need him to do a better job of showing me he loves me. What if he can't? The better question is: What if he won't? I need to know, not just believe in his love."

Abs took a second to think. "Men need to believe in themselves first, and sometimes it takes them awhile. I have a feeling your little separation has baptized Jake by fire and made him a believer."

I tilted my head. "I thought you were anti-husband."

She smirked. "Sugar, if Jake kisses anything like his brother, I wouldn't blame you one bit for running back to him."

My ovary popped an egg just thinking about his kisses. "You have no idea." I grabbed the railing for support. My knees went wobbly.

"Oh, I do. Just promise me you'll make him come running to you."

"Deal." I fanned myself.

Without saying another word, I opened the door a hair to make sure we didn't have any company. By the sound of it, all the company was partying below. When I didn't see anyone, we slipped into the foyer area of the master bedroom wing. It was as hoity-toity as it sounded. The foyer mimicked a hotel lobby, complete with chandelier and a blue velvet couch. Abs and I both shook our heads at the ridiculousness of it.

"One more door," I whispered.

Abs pulled her tension wrench and pick out of her pocket with the look of a mad scientist eager to experiment.

We crept across the foyer and landed in front of the dead bolted door. Who dead bolts their bedroom?

"What do you think they're hiding?" I asked in hushed tones while Abs worked her magic.

"Not sure, but it must be NSFW."

"Is that some type of code for, like, chains and whips?"

Abs patted my head. "You sweet, naive thing. It means not safe for work, and that's exactly what I'm talking about. Get ready to cover your eyes," she teased.

"Please hurry," I begged. I felt so exposed out in the open.

"I'm getting there, sugar." She twisted and turned her tools, smiled, and cussed.

Meanwhile, my eyes darted around. They landed on a huge life-size portrait of Vivian and Beau on the wall farthest from us. How I'd missed that walking in, I had no idea. Though now I would never be able to unsee it. Vivian was wearing a long silver gown with a slit up to her nether regions and was draped all over Beau, who was in a tux. He looked like a bronzed statue. Sure, he was gorgeous, but it was the shiny kind, not the real kind like Jake. Jake's beauty was more than skin deep.

I heard a click and whipped my head back to Abs, who was grinning.

"I love you."

"I know." She opened the door.

We both peeked in expecting to see some X-rated material, but all that was visible by the light of our phones was a froufrou room and a humongous bed dripping in cream satin with a blue velvet headboard to match the couch in the foyer. I had the urge to jump on it, but I zeroed in on the entire reason for this escapade. There sat my picture on Vivian's nightstand. I could see lipstick marks on the glass as if she'd kissed it goodnight one too many times. That fired me up.

I marched over, on white carpet so plush I was sinking into it, to snag the picture. I held it up and smiled at Jake and my baby before wiping it against my pant leg, trying to get the stain of Vivian off it.

Abs took my hand. "You can do that later. Let's get out of here."

Right.

We turned to leave when a voice drifted down the hall, putting the fear of God in us. Abs and I looked at each other with wide eyes. What was Vivian doing up here?

"What do we do?" I mouthed.

We both looked around the room in a panic. Vivian wasn't alone.

"Vivian, you're being ridiculous. Will you just come back to the party?" Beau asked, exasperated.

"No. Marla made me look like a fool out there," Vivian's shrill voice echoed.

"I told you we shouldn't have done this show. You're ruining our family's name," Beau growled.

"Me? You're down there drinking like a fish and hitting on anyone in a skirt under twenty-five," she roared.

"What about Jake?" he mocked.

"Oh please, you know that was for ratings. Why would I want some car salesman?"

JENNIFER PEEL

"Because you're jealous of his wife and he's the only man to ever tell you no. Something I should have learned to do a long time ago."

"Me? Jealous of Kasie?" she scoffed.

"You heard me right. For years you've bad-mouthed her even though you haven't seen her since high school, and she doesn't run in the same circles we do. I never understood why until recently. She got the toy you wanted to play with."

"You, you," she cried. "You have no idea what you're talking about."

"I wish I didn't."

"What is that supposed to mean?" Vivian raged.

"Only that you're not the woman I thought you were."

Abs and I looked at each other, stunned by the conversation and the fact that we were probably seconds away from getting busted. Even so, their little tiff explained a lot and made me more determined to save our own family's name.

"Me!" Vivian yelled. "If it wasn't for me, we wouldn't have half the business we have."

"Money is highly overrated," he threw back at her.

"So are you," she retorted.

"Let's just go back downstairs," Beau sounded defeated. "Please."

"Fine, but only because I need to have a word with Faye, the outreach coordinator for the hospital."

I breathed a silent sigh of relief.

"There you two are," another voice interrupted. It

sounded like the same voice I'd heard off camera in the video X had sent me.

"Can you please turn the camera off?" Beau begged.

"This is what you signed up for, buddy." The unidentified woman had no mercy.

"Whatever," Beau said. "We were just going back downstairs."

"I want to freshen up," Vivian interjected.

I grabbed Abs, my heart beating out of control.

"You look fine," Beau sighed.

"Ugh," she groaned. "Leave me be." Vivian sounded like a spoiled brat.

I pointed to what looked like the door to a closet. Abs and I sprinted for it. We flew inside and closed the door as quietly as we could. I was hugging the picture to me, unable to breathe. Then I realized I had the picture. Oh crap. Vivian wouldn't notice, right? Maybe it wouldn't matter one way or another—she was for sure going to notice the freaking motion sensor light that popped on in the closet.

Abs didn't seem as worried as me. She was looking all around us, mesmerized. It was becoming clear why Vivian didn't want anyone to come up here and why she kept her room dead bolted. The closet was like a dirty little secret. Vivian had a row of hair extensions hanging up. A cubby of fake eyelashes. SPANX and push-up bras for every occasion and more junk food than Publix. Miss I Never Eat Carbs or Sugar and I Don't Have Hair Extensions was a big fat liar.

Abs started snapping pictures with her phone like crazy.

"Stop it," I mouthed.

Abs waved me away and kept on snapping. "Leverage," she mouthed back.

I shook my head at her, though it wasn't a bad thought.

She stopped, though, when we heard Vivian shriek, "Why is our door unlocked?"

HELLO KITTY! We were so, so busted.

"Calm down. I think I forgot to lock it after I came up to get my cuff links," Beau said.

Bless Beau.

"I told you to be careful," she scolded him like he was a child.

No wonder Beau slept in the nanny quarters.

"Just hurry. People will start talking about why we left." He seemed nervous. Poor guy.

"I'll take as long as I need." Vivian was such a diva.

I prayed she didn't need some added extensions or a little snack. I also hoped that with the light on in the bedroom, she wouldn't notice the one in the closet. Although she did notice something.

"Who took my picture?" she howled.

"Someone stole the picture?" The unidentified woman sounded way too happy.

"As we told you before, no one, including the crew, is allowed to come in this room," Beau sounded like he was trying to contain the situation.

I hoped that meant they would all leave, maybe try to find the culprit downstairs, but then a bad, bad thing happened.

"There are shoe prints in the carpet leading to the closet," Vivian roared. "I'm going to kill someone."

Oops. I was dead.

Chapter Nine

VIVIAN THREW OPEN THE closet door with fire in her violet eyes. Which I'm pretty sure were much more vibrant due to the colored contacts I'd seen near the fake eyelashes. Everything about her was fake, except perhaps the fury she was exuding. I'd never seen anyone's nostrils flare so big. I mean, like, wow. She might have even been able to shove a super-size tampon up one.

"Hi, Vivian," I sang and held up the frame. What else could I do? "Just came by to get the picture you borrowed." I gave a her a sickly sweet smile.

"Jake's wife is here?" The unknown woman sounded like she'd won the lottery. "Get the cameras in here."

No. No. No.

Vivian panicked, grabbing me and Abs, yanking us out of her closet, and slamming the door shut. Before anything could be said or Abs and I could run for it, there was a camera crew in place. It was kind of scary. We're talking lights, camera, action.

I was finally able to put a face to the voice. A quite

short woman in stilettos with a blunt blonde haircut was directing everyone before she turned her sights on me. Her smile reminded me of the Grinch when he decided to steal Christmas. I actually reached for my heart. I had a feeling she could rip it out of my chest while it was still beating.

Beau took a protective stance in front of Vivian, Abs, and me. "Tera,"—I'm assuming she was the Grinch—"there's nothing to see here. Our friends were just leaving."

Beau was my new favorite person.

Tera arched her left brow so high I thought it might stick like that. "Do your friends normally steal things from you?"

I bravely stepped to the side so I could look Tera in the eye. "Excuse me, I didn't steal anything." I held up the picture. "This belongs to me and my husband, but you already knew that."

"Did I?" she said as if daring me to contradict her. "As far as I know, your husband gifted that to Vivian. Isn't that right, Vivian?"

Vivian's cheeks flushed for half a second before she stepped out and straightened her tiny black cocktail dress. "Of course."

I glared at Vivian. "Jake would have never given you this photo."

"You don't know your husband very well," she spat back.

Those were fighting words, but I realized I was on camera. "Tera, is it? You don't have permission to film me. I know I would have to sign a waiver of some sort."

Her smug, tight-from-plastic-surgery face dropped.

"Great." Beau clapped his hands together. "We'll see you later, Kasie and friend."

I grabbed Abs, ready to hightail it out of there.

"Wait." Tera held out her hand like a crossing guard trying to stop traffic. "Don't you think you should call the police, Vivian?"

I swallowed down my heart, lungs, and everything I'd eaten last week.

"We're not calling the police," Beau stated matter-of-factly.

"Vivian, are you sure?" Tera coaxed. "I mean, these women violated your home." Tera gave me the sleaziest smile. "And she's accusing you of lying." Tera was what my momma would call a pot stirrer.

Abs gripped my hand. I could feel her shaking next to me. I felt awful for getting her mixed up in this. I was shaking, too, but with outrage. Tera was a piece of work.

Vivian's eyes darted between me, Beau, and Tera. Beau was shaking his head as if to beg her not to listen to Tera. Vivian honestly looked torn, tugging on her polyester hair.

Tera wasn't going to give up. "Think about what that *picture* means to you," she emphasized.

Tera had said the magic words, making Vivian stand tall and proud. "You're right; we should call the authorities." Vivian smirked at me.

Abs nudged me as if I should say something to get us out of this. The only thing I could think of was, "Go ahead—I have proof Vivian lied and stole the picture."

"Sure you do." Tera wasn't buying it.

"Do you want to see it?" I wasn't backing down. Daddy always said making someone believe you was more about confidence than the truth.

All eyes were on me, and if I wasn't mistaken, Beau's were begging me not to show anyone anything. It suddenly became clear to me who X was. Dang it.

"There's nothing to see." Vivian's brows furrowed, yet her voice quavered.

Tera rubbed the back of her neck as if she were worried too, then she quickly recovered. "Hmm. Let's see what you have."

Beau coughed and I swore I heard the word *don't* in there.

I was sure if I revealed the video I had, he would probably get in some sort of legal trouble. However, if I didn't, I would find myself and Abs in the same trouble. "Well." I cleared my throat. "Um, I can't right now because . . ." I was an idiot.

Tera and Vivian's slimy smiles at my obvious stalling lit a fire under me and gave me an idea I prayed would work.

"I can't because it's at Jake's office," I rushed to say.

Vivian and Tera rolled their eyes.

They only emboldened me. "I bet you didn't know Jake has a security camera in his office." I was sure they didn't, because he didn't. Regardless, that wiped the smiles right off their smug faces.

"Yep," I sang. "I saw you take the photo while he was getting your car keys."

"That's just pre ... preposterous," Vivian stuttered.

"Is it?"

Vivian looked to Tera to answer.

Tera stepped closer to me, sizing me up as she went. When she landed next to me, she looked me over from head to toe. "There's no reason we can't all be friends here."

"Right," Abs scoffed.

Tera shot her a lethal look. "Listen, ladies, you were caught red-handed tonight, and if we call the police you will leave here in handcuffs. Now, no one wants that."

Sure, she didn't. She was salivating at the thought of us being taken into custody.

"And while you say you have some sort of proof that Vivian took the photo," she continued, "we have plenty of lawyers who will make sure that security footage never sees the light of day."

Hello Kitty. I hated this woman.

"So, I propose a deal." She flipped her hair.

"Deal?" I questioned.

"A deal of a lifetime," she said, so dang cockily before pressing her lips together. "So, this is what I propose. The Jenningses, out of the goodness of their hearts, won't call the police and press charges. In exchange, you will destroy any said video you claim to have and ... you will agree to let us air footage from tonight of your little caper, as well as you returning your beloved photo to Jake."

My eyes widened. "What? How do you even know I was going to give it back to him?"

"Oh, honey, don't play coy with me. I know." She poked my chest with her long red nail. "And depending on how our viewers react, you might need to appear on a few more episodes."

"You're crazy. I have no desire to be on your toxic show."

"Aww, what a pity," she used a baby voice. "I guess we'll be calling the police and suing you for the video you have."

"Kasie," Abs whispered, "how bad could it be?" She pulled me back and away from Looney Tunes and whispered even lower, "I could lose my job if I get arrested."

I looked into Abs's eyes, and reality sunk deep in the pit of my stomach. I couldn't let Abs take the fall for my pride. I closed my eyes. "Fine," I breathed out.

When I opened my eyes, Tera gave me the smirkiest of smirks. "You made the right choice. Welcome to the family." She snapped her fingers. "Kyle, get me some release forms and coffee, pronto."

Before I could catch my breath and think about what I'd just agreed to, all the other wives showed up looking shiny. I'd never seen so many sequins. I needed sunglasses.

Marla waltzed in, in all her blazing red hair glory. "What's going on in here?"

"No one is supposed to be in here." Vivian waved her hands around, flustered.

"Please," Marla said, "we all know you really use extensions and have a stockpile of junk food."

Vivian's jaw dropped, but all she could do was splutter.

Beau walked out of the room, obviously disgusted with how things had turned out. He wasn't the only one. I wanted to apologize to him and thank him for trying to help me.

Abs snickered at Marla's comment, drawing attention to us.

Marla and the other wives—Pauline, Roxanne, Elsie, and Heather—all headed our way. Their doe eyes made it look as if they were five-year-old girls heading into the pet store to check out the cute puppies on display. The glittery babes surrounded us as if they were going to bedazzle us and make us become one of them. Or maybe perform a satanic ritual. Perhaps they could cast away the unrelenting nausea that was bubbling inside of me. What had I done? How was Jake going to feel about all of this? I clutched the picture tighter to me. It was worth it, right?

"I love your jumpsuits," Elsie, the wife of country singer superstar Owen Patton, raved. "Where did you get them?" She reached out with her tiny hands and touched my sleeve. She was the youngest wife, practically a child bride. I related to her struggles the most on the show. The other wives made fun of her all the time for getting married so young.

"I made them."

The wives in unison all said, "Really?"

"She owns her own online boutique," Abs jumped in with a big grin.

"How did we not know this?" Marla quipped.

"Could you make me one in pink?" Elsie asked. She was known for her pink obsession on the show. Her bedroom was covered in it. Owen didn't seem to mind. He had a one-track mind and as long as his wife shared his bed, he didn't care what color it was.

"Um . . . sure," I responded, not able to think. I felt like I was dreaming, and I desperately wanted to wake up from this nightmare.

Elsie clapped her hands together and squealed.

Heather pulled her phone out of her bra. "What's the name of your boutique?"

"Maribelle and Me."

Heather tapped and typed a few things before pulling up my website. Before I knew it, she was oohing and aahing at my designs and showing them to the other wives, who all seemed impressed. Except for one wife—Vivian. She had moseyed on over with her nose so stuck up in the air it was a good thing it wasn't raining or she would have drowned, especially with how wide her nostrils could go. I was surprised I'd never noticed that back in high school. I think I had been too intimidated by her then. I had always felt like I lived in her shadow. If I'd only known how thin her veneer really was, I could have stepped into the light. I supposed I had tonight, except I didn't want it to be the limelight.

"How precious are those Sunday dresses?" Vivian did her thing—the thing where she wanted everyone to think it was a compliment, but you could hear the sarcasm weave its way into every syllable.

Marla gave her the stink eye, not at all buying her load of crap. "Jealous much?"

Vivian slapped a hand against her chest as if she had been mortally wounded. She loved playing the victim. "I'm not jealous of her," she stumbled on her words.

All the other wives laughed.

Pauline rested a hand on Vivian's bare shoulder. "Please, honey; you're practically green with envy. She has everything you want."

Vivian tsked, her facade weakening. "Please. She makes mommy-and-me dresses and is separated from her car salesman husband."

Marla zeroed in on the picture I was holding like a security blanket. "I thought you loved Jake?"

"Well ... well," Vivian spluttered. "It's complicated."

Marla wagged her brows. "I bet it is. Don't worry, though; I have a feeling a reunion is about to take place between Jake and this gorgeous little thing."

I wasn't so sure about that. Jake was probably going to flip his lid when I told him what I'd done and that I'd gotten him involved. He hated reality TV more than I did. However, I didn't voice my concerns. Vivian scoffed so hard she'd probably coughed up half her lung. That only egged on the pride monster living inside of me.

I batted my real eyelashes and put one hand behind my back, crossing my fingers and silently praying. "Get ready for a dazzling reunion."

Chapter ten

MY THUMB OVERED OVER the green call button. I knew I needed to tell Jake what had happened tonight even though it was close to midnight. Dallas, after he'd died of laughter, had promised he wouldn't say anything. Though I doubted Dallas had gone home. He and Abs had dropped me off and practically kicked me out of the car. They were off to do whatever, though I'd bet grits were involved based on the way they were making out at every red light. They had gotten so exuberant; I'd threatened to walk home. I hoped Abs knew what she was getting into. I loved Dallas, but he was a heartbreaker.

I had my own heartbreak to worry about, though, and a little matter that included me looking like a fool next week on national TV. After I'd signed my life away, that terror, Tera, had made Abs and me reenact coming out of that closet with the photo and being caught by Vivian. At least I got to call Vivian a liar. Who knew whether they would show that or not. They obviously did a lot of editing.

I sank into the couch, and with a loud exhale, I

pushed the button. It rang only once before Jake answered.

"Kasie, is everything all right?" He sounded worried.

That was a good question. I didn't know how to answer. When I took too long to respond, Jake, in a panic, said, "Baby, are you there?" He hadn't called me baby in so long I started to cry. And the sound of his voice, after the night I'd had, did something to me. He used to be my best friend, and I missed him. I needed him to make it better.

"I'm here," I croaked through the tears.

"What's wrong? Is Maribelle okay?" his voice begged for me to say yes. Maribelle was the apple of his eye.

"Yes. She's fine."

"Kasie," he said tenderly, "tell me what you need." He had no idea how much I wanted to hear those words. It was like we were young again and he could read my mind.

"Jake, I did something stupid tonight."

"It can't be that bad."

"Oh, it's bad."

"Whatever it is, we'll fix it. Just tell me."

Where was this Jake six months ago? That didn't matter right now.

"So . . . I broke into the Jennings' place and took the picture Vivian stole from you," I rushed to say.

Jake was so silent, I thought he'd hung up, but then he started to laugh.

"It's not funny. Abs and I got caught by that liar, Vivian, and one of the evil producers made me agree to let them film the entire embarrassing thing. If I didn't, they were going to call the police. I was all for getting arrested, but I couldn't do that to Abs. And now the whole world is going to know what I did," I whined.

"This is the best news I've heard in a long time." Jake sounded way more chipper about this than I'd been expecting.

"How can you say that? I'm going to humiliate our family."

"Kasie, you just gave me reason to hope."

I sat up, confused. "Hope for what?"

"Us," he whispered. "There's no way in hell the girl I know would have gone to the trouble unless she believed me."

I grabbed a throw pillow and clung to it. "Jake, I need to apologize to you. Someone sent me the video of what really happened at the dealership that day. I'm sorry for accusing you of cheating on me and for all the awful things people have been saying about you."

"I don't blame you. I deserve it all. But who sent you the video?" He sounded disappointed that I hadn't come to the conclusion he wasn't a liar on my own.

I told him about X, who I was sure was Beau, but mentioned we couldn't tell anyone. I went into detail of the entire night's events, and then I added in, "Also, I had to promise Tera they could film me giving you back the picture. I know I shouldn't have spoken for you, but I was kind of under duress and—"

"Kasie," he interrupted. "I'll do anything you need me to do."

"You will?" I wanted to kiss him for it.

"You're my wife. I would do anything for you."

Tears streamed down my face. "I want to believe that."

"The part about you being my wife or that I would do anything for you?"

I curled into myself. "Both."

He paused for a moment. "I know I promised you I would stay away and never hurt you again, but Kasie, I love you. I don't want to live without you. I'll do whatever I have to do to prove that to you."

I wanted that more than anything—to believe in him again. "Well, you're going to get your shot on national TV."

He chuckled. "Bring it on."

"FYI, you're going to need to put a security camera in your office."

"What? Why?"

"Let's just say I may have fudged the truth a bit tonight."

"I wish I could have seen that."

"You'll be able to. Just tune in next week."

"I'd like to watch it with you ... if you're amenable." He sounded like the boy who was nervous to ask me on a first date.

I bit my lip. "That depends."

"On what?"

"How convincing you are when I give you your picture back."

"Baby, get the popcorn ready."

Tera was the most demanding woman on the planet. She insisted we film our part on Sunday so they could work it into the show before it aired in the coming week. Maybe that was a good thing. We could get all the embarrassing stuff out of the way in one fell swoop. Although it meant Jake hustling to get a security camera installed in his office and us facing each other. Getting the camera installed was the easy part.

It's not that I didn't want to see Jake. I did. Still, I was nervous. We had a lot of issues that needed to be ironed out, and I didn't want to open the ironing board in front of the entire world. What if we couldn't iron out all the wrinkles in our relationship? What if our irons no longer burned for each other the way they used to? Or what if they heated up only to get unplugged again? I really needed to quit comparing our marriage to a household chore.

Regardless, it was either get arrested or make a fool of myself on TV. Jake said he'd do his part. I had to trust that—him. If I didn't, there was no hope for us, and my heart couldn't take that thought.

Abs and Dallas wanted to be there. They had apparently spent the entire weekend together. I didn't even want to know what they had been doing. Though I had a pretty good guess. Maribelle also wanted in on the action. She'd driven home yesterday. I was always happy to have her home, and I was especially eager to have her now when the house seemed so quiet. I'd never felt so alone.

I was grateful to have Maribelle's company on the

drive over to the dealership, which was typically closed on Sundays, but Jake's uncle Ray was more than happy to open up the doors for today's filming. Even though Jake had gotten bad press, Ray had seen a bump in business and that's all that mattered to him. It was all that ever mattered to him. He couldn't have cared less about Jake's feelings. To him, Jake was only another minion.

Maribelle sat tall and perky in the passenger seat, looking so grown up with her hair in a messy bun and wearing the cashmere sweater I'd gotten her for Christmas and the designer jeans her daddy always made sure she had the money to buy.

"Do you think I can get on camera too?" Maribelle checked her lip gloss in the visor mirror.

"Darlin', this isn't exactly something we want to be on. You realize how fake reality TV is, right?"

She gave me her signature sweet smile. "Momma, haven't you heard there's no such thing as bad publicity? We learned that in my marketing class."

"We don't need publicity."

"Sure you do. Look at all the new orders you already got. I bet you get even more next week." Her beautiful blue eyes lit up.

"I don't think I can handle any more. I'll have to hire some new people."

"See. You always wanted your own store. Maybe this will help. You know, after you and Daddy make up," she pleaded.

I would love to have my own storefront one day. Jake had always promised me we would make it happen. But it wasn't a cheap endeavor, and college tuition was expensive. Then there was the little matter of us separating. I patted Maribelle's leg. "Baby girl, you know there's no guarantee."

"I know," she sighed. "But Daddy loves you, and he's really sorry for being so stupid. He's changing, Momma. He didn't even get mad when I told him Rhett came down to Tuscaloosa to see me last week. He said he'd overreacted when we were in high school."

I whipped my head her way. "He did? Why didn't you tell me?" I focused back on the road. Jake had always been adamant that Maribelle graduate from college before she even thought about Rhett again.

"Because you've been so sad about Daddy, it didn't seem right for me to be happy."

"Maribelle, I always want your happiness."

"I want yours, too, Momma . . . and Daddy's. I know you're not happy apart." Her eyes got misty. "One of my favorite memories growing up is when I was twelve and I got my tonsils out. I remember waking up in the middle of the night while I was sleeping on the couch. You and Daddy were watching over me. Daddy was holding you on the overstuffed chair. I heard him whisper, 'You and Maribelle are my world. How did I ever get so lucky?'"

My eyes watered. "I didn't know you'd heard that."

"Well," she smiled, "I had to pretend I wasn't awake because Daddy started kissing you after that, and it grossed me out."

I laughed. "Sorry we grossed you out."

"I'm not. I always knew you loved each other,

even when things got weird between you before I left for college."

"Baby girl." I let out a heavy breath. "Things haven't been right for a while."

"Yeah, but there's still time to fix it," she said with all her beautiful heart.

"I have hope. We'll have to see how good of an actor your daddy is today," I teased.

"Momma, he doesn't have to act. He loves you. I know he does."

I tightened my grip on the steering wheel. That was my greatest hope.

Chapter Eleven

I WAITED OUTSIDE OF Jake's office at the dealership—
not because I wanted to, but because Tera didn't want
me to see Jake until I walked in bearing the picture,
which Tera had made her assistant wrap in gold
wrapping paper. Honestly, reality TV was the biggest
oxymoron in the world. There was nothing real about
it. But I kept my mouth shut because I didn't want a
police record. Though I did keep an eye on the picture
and the assistant. That picture was going back where it
belonged.

There was a flurry of activity inside and outside
of Jake's office. They were switching out lights and
even moving around the office furniture, from the
sound of it. Meanwhile, Maribelle was talking to Marla
and Elsie, who had come to lend support. Not sure
why. I hardly knew them, but they warned me that
Vivian was about to get real ugly. It might have had
something to do with Abs texting Marla the pictures
she'd taken of Vivian's closet. I think Abs and Marla
were on their way to having a beautiful relationship
based on their mutual dislike for Vivian. That was, if

JENNIFER PEEL

Dallas could keep his hands off Abs for more than five seconds at a time. I'd never seen him so handsy, and that was saying something. Abs didn't seem to mind at all. She was glowing and hung on his every word. I feared for her. She was under the Baldwin spell.

Jake's uncle was passing out his business card to everyone and offering test drives. Most people didn't look twice at his card, yet Ray rambled on and on about what a good deal he could give them. It was as embarrassing as his comb-over that I'd been dying to cut for the last ten years.

Before I was allowed to go into the office, Elsie and Marla, along with Maribelle, approached me while I was pacing the tiled checkered floor and taking in the new car smell that permeated the building.

"Momma," Maribelle gushed while reaching for my hand. "Marla and Elsie and I were just talking, and they love all the pictures of us together on your website."

"You're like the most gorgeous-looking sisters ever," Elsie sang. "I can't believe you are old enough to be her momma."

Well, I *was* barely old enough, but yeah. "You're too kind."

"Kind has nothing to do with it," Marla said. "We speak the truth."

Maribelle couldn't hold in whatever excitement was building up inside of her. "Which is why Elsie thinks we should be in her husband's new music video," she squealed.

"Oh yes," Elsie dreamily sighed. "You would be perfect. His new single coming out in the spring is

102

about a momma's love. And the pictures of you two say it all."

"She said we could even wear some of your designs, Momma," Maribelle could hardly contain herself.

I blinked a million times, trying to take it all in. "I don't know. I'm not an actress and—"

Marla waved her hand in front of me. "Oh, honey, you put on quite the show Friday night. Believe me, you'll do just fine. And think about how much it will irritate Vivian," she said evilly.

As fun as that sounded, I honestly wanted to be done with Vivian. This was all too surreal for me. "I'll have to think about it."

"Come on, Momma," Maribelle begged before she snuggled up to me. "You're the prettiest, sweetest momma ever."

I kissed her cheek. "And you are the most beautiful con artist ever."

Everyone laughed.

Tera, dressed to kill in tight leather pants and a jacket to match, interrupted the lighthearted moment with her no-nonsense attitude. "It's time." She shoved the wrapped picture into my hands.

"You got this." Marla winked.

Elsie patted my arm. "Think about the offer. We'll talk later."

I nodded before giving Maribelle a squeeze for comfort and courage.

"Good luck, Momma." Maribelle waved and walked away.

I smoothed out my gray sweater dress; it had a bit

of a plunging neckline and showed off my curves. I'd probably gone overboard on the outfit, but I wanted to look good for the millions of people who would be watching me humiliate myself. Really, though, it was all for Jake. Especially the romantic updo that had a few tendrils left loose, framing my heart-shaped face. He loved my hair like that. A long time ago, he loved it even more when his hands could run through it and destroy it in a matter of passionate seconds. I'd loved that too.

"Just behave like you normally would," Tera barked.

Like that was possible. There were absolutely zero things normal about this. I couldn't even respond to her. I let out a heavy breath.

"Oh, and make sure you dazzle us, like you promised." There was a razor-sharp edge to her sultry voice.

Why did I ever say that? Actually, why did I ever break into Vivian's house? I looked at Maribelle giggling and chatting it up with Elsie and Marla and I knew why. It was about the truth. And my baby deserved for the world to know that her daddy wasn't a lying cheating loser. Jake deserved that too. And maybe it was a bit about my pride. Or a lot. Regardless, I was as nervous as a tick, which was ridiculous. Jake had held my hair back when I vomited and changed the bedsheets when my periods got crazy at night. He knew I had stretch marks from giving birth and cellulite on my upper thighs that would never go away. Yet, I still was trembling.

I refused to show my fear to Tera. "Get your

sunglasses ready. You're going to be dazzled like never before." Wow. I was losing it.

She narrowed her dark eyes at me. "We'll see." She threw open the office door and swept in like a tornado before slamming it shut. I was supposed to knock. You know, all in the name of this being normal behavior.

"Go Kasie!" Dallas yelled.

That made me smile as I raised my curled fist, preparing to knock on Jake's door. It was only a few minutes of my life, I kept telling myself. I closed my eyes for a second and mustered up some courage before finally knocking.

It didn't take Jake long to say, "Come in."

I clutched the picture to me and opened the door. When I peeked in, I hardly recognized the place, and maybe I should have worn sunglasses. So many lights. Jake sat up straight at his desk. I noticed he had dressed up more than he normally would for work. He was wearing his charcoal suit coat and the blue tie I'd bought him last year for Easter to wear to church. He quite honestly took my breath away.

Jake popped up, his eyes bright and his smile only for me. "Kasie," he sounded surprised. He was a better actor than I thought.

"Hi, Jake," I whispered, shy because of our audience and because, for some reason, I saw the boy I'd fallen in love with who'd promised he would always be mine—not the man who had let me walk out the door. It all felt so new. Too bad I could see the cameraman closing in on me in my peripheral vision.

Oh well, I was here to dazzle. "I brought you something." I stepped closer.

Jake looked me over from head to toe. His grin turned more seductive. I knew that grin. I missed it. And he knew it was reeling me right in. Except he didn't make me come to him—he stepped around his desk and rushed to me. Suddenly, no one else existed in that room. Jake enveloped my senses, from his musky cologne to the way his baby blues held my gaze. Oh, how I ached to reach up and run my hand through his tousled curls, then graze his stubbled cheeks with my fingers.

"You look amazing." He gently played with one of the tendrils around my face.

"You look great too." I handed him the wrapped picture. "I thought you might like this back."

He didn't take the frame. No. He did something totally unexpected. He wrapped his arms around me, smashing the picture between us. With me in heeled boots, we were almost face-to-face.

His warm, minty breath played between us and tickled my skin while his lips hovered above mine. "I only want one thing back," he whispered.

"What's that?" I stuttered, hardly able to breathe. Jake was literally stealing my breath in the best sort of way.

He leaned in a little closer and barely brushed my lips. "You, Kasie. Only you." He crushed my lips with his own.

Hello Kitty. His warm lips felt like home and everything good in the world. When he parted my own, I died and went to heaven, and probably popped two eggs. He tasted like peppermint hot chocolate with whipped cream—hot and sweet. Each sweep of his tongue soothed my soul and had me melting right into him. He certainly hadn't lost his touch. But before I begged him to come home with me and take me to our bed, I pulled away. Sex was always the easy part—a Band-Aid, even. We needed superglue.

"Jake," I stuttered, so overcome by him.

The back of his hand glided down my tear-stained cheek while his eyes searched my own. "I know, Kasie. We'll take it step by step." Wow, he was good at reading my mind.

"I'd like that. So much."

He kissed my brow and chuckled low. "Did you have something you wanted to give me?"

I snuggled against him, still holding his "gift." "I'm good with this."

"Give him the picture," Tera hissed.

Ugh. She broke the Baldwin spell. I hated her. Fine. I leaned away. "This belongs to you." I handed him the picture. This time he took it. "I want you to know that I believe you." I had imagined me saying what a liar Vivian was, but I found, in the moment, it didn't matter. All I cared about was Jake and our family.

He unwrapped the picture, letting the wrapping paper fall to the floor. He smiled while his fingers brushed across the glass. "I remember this day like it was yesterday."

"Me too. She always wanted you to push her higher and higher on the swing."

Jake looked up from the picture. "Just like her beautiful momma. Thank you, Kasie. I love you."

"I love you too," fell out of my mouth so naturally.

"That's a wrap," Tera shouted, ruining the moment.

I let out a sigh of relief that it was over but was irritated that she'd interrupted us.

Tera walked toward us, clapping. "Well. Well. Well. You do know how to dazzle. I think we all might need a cold shower after that kiss. Nicely done, you two. You almost made me a believer in true love. Almost," she cackled. "Anyway, you'll be hearing from me. And remember, I stand between you and a criminal record." She looked up to the security camera. "I'm going to need that footage of Vivian, by the way."

Jake folded his arms. "I don't think so. I talked to our attorney. He looked through the contracts we signed with you, and you have no right to any security footage."

Whoa, he was attractive when he got all protective and businesslike.

Tera's jaw dropped. "Excuse me. That's not how this works."

Jake smirked at her. "I think it is. And I suggest that you don't harass my wife anymore."

I had never been more in love with him, and if we weren't in a room full of people, I would have showed him how much. It was probably a good thing I couldn't. We needed the superglue, not the Band-Aid.

Jake took my hand, and we walked toward the door.

"You'll be hearing from me," Tera roared.

"We'll be busy," Jake tossed back.

Yes. Very busy. We had a relationship to fix.

Chapter twelve

MOMMA GLARED AT JAKE from the kitchen. "I don't know how I feel about you giving him a second chance," she whispered.

My gaze drifted toward Jake, who was standing in our family room laughing with Dallas and Abs. Several of our other friends mingled about our open floor plan; even Jake's parents were there. We were having a *Wives of Nashville* watch party. I mean, I was going to be embarrassed, so we figured I should be humiliated among friends and family. Besides, it was nice to do something fun as a couple. You know, other than being on TV.

I rested the knife I was using, to slice peppers for the dip garnish, on the counter and wrapped an arm around Momma. "I know, Momma. I'm scared too, but I'm more afraid not to try."

She leaned her head on mine. "You two were always like a pig to mud."

I leaned away with a grimace. "I'm not sure I like that analogy."

She laughed and tapped my nose. "You know

what I mean. And if you were a pig, you would be the prettiest one of the bunch."

I rolled my eyes. "Thanks, Momma. I think."

"Don't get your knickers all twisted. All I'm saying is that I knew the boy was trouble when he walked in the house for the first time. You looked at him as if you'd seen the light and were having a holy experience. It was the same way I looked at your daddy," she choked up.

I patted her arm. "Is that a bad thing?"

"No," she conceded. "But you make sure he treats you the way I know he can."

"I will," I promised.

Jake appeared in the kitchen. "What can I help with?"

Momma gave Jake a shrewd stare while picking up the charcuterie board she'd been working on. "Look who showed up."

Jake's chest rose and fell noticeably. He knew convincing my momma would be tougher than proving to me he was worthy of another shot. "Jo . . . Mom." He gave her a sheepish grin. He rarely called her Mom. "I know it's only lip service right now, but I am sorry. I promise to do right by Kasie."

Momma narrowed her eyes, her crow's feet taking center stage. "You see that you do, Jake Baldwin." She marched off in a huff toward the table we'd set up in the family room for the food.

Jake watched her go and sighed. "Do you think she'll ever forgive me?"

"Eventually."

Jake grabbed my blouse and tugged me closer. "How about you? Will you forgive me?"

"Eventually," I sang with a smile.

He grinned before kissing my lips. "I'll take what I can get. How can I help you?"

I'd always loved that Jake wasn't one of those guys who thought he needed to be waited on. Even when he wasn't as attentive as I'd wanted him to be, he always helped out around the house.

"Can you taste this?" I pointed at the dip. "I'm too nervous to eat."

"Baby, it's going to be fine."

"You know how they edit things. And I broke into someone's house." I cringed. In hindsight, I couldn't believe I'd ever thought that was a great idea.

Jake brushed back my hair, which I had done in long wavy curls. "Kasie, you amaze me. This is going to be a great story to tell our grandchildren one day."

I tilted my head. "Funny. You've never talked about grandbabies before." I had to admit I loved the sound of it. You know, in like twenty years when I was old enough to be someone's mimi, or gigi, or something besides grandma. I was still young enough to have my own babies.

"I don't like to think about Maribelle growing up, but I do want to grow old with you."

I rested my hand on his stubbled cheek. "That might be one of the sweetest things you have ever said to me."

He leaned in and nuzzled my ear. "I have more sweet things to say."

"Like what?" I breathed out. Hello Kitty, he was good at getting my pulse up.

"Like I want to—"

"Hey, you two, it's about to start," Abs interrupted us.

Never before had I wanted to throw her a crusty look. I needed to hear what Jake wanted to do. I had a feeling it was going to be good. Still, I couldn't be rude to my best friend, who was gleaming like a brand-new Cadillac. She and Dallas were still, uh, well, I assumed enjoying grits, though we were under strict don't ask, don't tell protocols. I loved them both, but it was best I didn't know the gory details. Especially because I knew it wasn't going to last and was going to get all sorts of awkward.

Jake groaned in my ear before standing up straight.

Abs wagged her brows at us. "You can canoodle later. Let's watch us make fools of ourselves."

I buried my head into Jake's shoulder. "Do we have to?"

Jake kissed my head. "Come on. I'm looking forward to this."

"Ugh. I'm glad someone is."

He took my hand and led us around our large island and into the family room. All eyes were on us. I'm sure everyone was wondering if Jake and I were going to make it. Jake was still staying with Dallas until we were sure we would stick. Until my heart trusted him. Don't get me wrong—I'd loved the last couple of days. It felt like falling in love all over again. But, I worried about when real life hit. Right now, we seemed to be in another honeymoon phase.

The love seat looked to be reserved for us, as no one was sitting in it. I felt bad since we had friends sitting on the floor and crowded onto our sofa and two overstuffed chairs. Although, if the smiles we received were any indication, no one seemed to mind. I should say the smiles we received from our friends—our parents were skeptical. With her bulldog stare, my momma looked to be reserving judgment, while Jake's parents whispered among themselves. I'd never been their favorite person. I wondered if they had been hoping we were truly over.

I would never forget the day we'd told his parents we were pregnant. It was as if I had stolen the sun. They weren't rich people by any means, but they'd worked hard their entire married life to save up for Jake to attend college and make his dreams of becoming a lawyer come true. We had naively told them we could still make it all happen. They'd laughed in our faces. Sometimes I wondered what would have happened if they had believed in us. I supposed it didn't matter now.

The show's theme music began. It had a country music flare to it. This was Nashville, after all—Music City. I snuggled up to Jake, getting ready to bury my head in his chest when I came on the screen. They started flashing scenes of the wives, and yes, even me, Abs, and Jake, while the show's female voice-over announcer said with a heavy drawl, "In tonight's episode, the wives hold a charity event, and ooh, there's a party crasher. You'll never guess who. And will Vivian and Jake rekindle their romance, or will Jake break her heart? Stay tuned for the wildest episode this season."

Even though I knew what a liar Vivian was, I squirmed, not liking the sound of how they were spinning the lies. I'd known they would sensationalize it, but they were going overboard.

Jake held on to me tight. "There was never anything to rekindle. I swear," he whispered in my ear.

Everyone turned to Jake and goaded him. None of our friends believed the crap being peddled by the show, but still Jake turned a shade of crimson. "The woman is psycho; you'll see," he pleaded anyway.

"Honestly, she is." I came to Jake's defense, even though I didn't really need to. But I'd already committed larceny on his behalf, so I might as well do a thorough job of clearing his name.

"Total nutjob," Abs added. She and Dallas were scrunched on the couch, though they didn't seem to mind, as Abs was on his lap. They were a cute couple. Maybe they could last. Maybe.

Everyone laughed and went back to watching the circus on TV.

I watched with one eye open. They started the show with the charity event. It was swanky. I hadn't gotten a look at it in person because Abs and I had sneaked out the way we had come in that night. They showed the wives mixing and mingling with Nashville's elite, including several country music stars I loved. Maybe I should have gone downstairs to check out the party, except I'd been way underdressed and a little frazzled.

Vivian was front and center. The show totally played her off as the victim. Marla asked her if Beau was moving on from her. The camera panned over to Beau, who was talking to a young woman in a stunning red dress. It didn't look like anything nefarious was going on. He wasn't even staring at her ample curves. In fact, they were talking about the real estate market. But Vivian, with tears in her eyes, marched on over and made a scene. The young woman turned as red as her dress and slinked away. Beau held his tongue, but the spiteful look he gave Vivian pricked my heart. He had obviously once cared for her. You couldn't loathe someone that way unless you had once loved them very much.

"I feel awful for him," I whispered to Jake.

"How could you ever think I would choose her over you?" he whispered back.

I sat up so we were eye to eye. "Because you asked her to homecoming first."

"Kasie Ann." He tucked some of my hair back. "I only asked her because Kaleb Rawlings said he'd already asked you and you'd accepted."

"Why would he say that? I flat out told him no." Kaleb was the most popular boy in school, and he knew it. He also had a reputation for taking girls out and not taking no for an answer. He and Vivian had actually ended up going together. The homecoming king and queen.

"When I figured that out, I broke the date off with Vivian."

My mouth dropped. "She said yes?"

He nodded.

"But she said she turned you down, and you never said anything to the contrary."

"Well," he shrugged, "I felt guilty for breaking the date with her, and she threw a hissy fit about it, so I told her she could tell whatever story she wanted. I didn't know you felt so threatened by her. If I had, I would have said something. All I cared about is that I got to go with the girl of my dreams."

I playfully smacked his chest. "You're laying it on thick."

He placed his hand over mine against his chest. "I'm telling the truth."

"Jake." I lowered my head. "I know I wasn't your dream."

He tipped my chin with his finger. "Kasie—"

Our friends erupted in cheers and clapping.

My head whipped toward the screen. There I was, live in living color with Abs in Vivian's closet. I sat on the edge of my seat, literally.

Jake sat up next to me. "We're going to finish that conversation." He kissed my cheek.

I knew we needed to. No more sweeping things under the rug; although, I knew the truth already, and I wasn't looking forward to the blow my heart would take. Plus, I worried whether we would be able to build new dreams together or not.

Tera made a big production of us "coming out of the closet." All the wives were there acting stunned and talking among themselves, except for Vivian, who threw her hand over her voluptuous chest. "Why would you do this?" she cried.

My face on-screen said exactly how I was feeling.

My nose wrinkled, and I rolled my eyes. "Please save your tears. We both know Jake never gave you this picture. I'm only taking back what's mine." There was a double meaning there.

"You're sexy all fired up," Jake said out loud.

"Shhh." Our friends said in unison, and Dallas threw popcorn at him.

I squinted. I hated watching myself on TV. This was so embarrassing.

When I called Vivian out, the other wives all looked at me as if I were their new hero.

Vivian, of course, acted like a wounded deer. "Are you calling me a liar?" she whined.

"Ding. Ding. Ding."

All the wives laughed.

Vivian threw them the vilest of looks before hitting me with her death stare. "We'll see who comes out laughing. The truth will be known." She swept out of the room dramatically.

Abs and I high-fived before it cut to the next scene.

There I was outside of Jake's office. They showed the entire scene, which was also embarrassing. Especially when our friends started hooting and hollering. I had to admit, though, we looked good together. I even got butterflies in my stomach watching us and remembering how good it felt to be in Jake's arms.

Jake in real life put his arm around me, and I rested my head on his shoulder. We could be each other's dreams, right?

"What got into you? You're not usually into PDA," I whispered.

"You said I needed to make it good if I wanted you to go out with me. And I thought maybe if I had shown the world more often how much you meant to me, you wouldn't have believed I would ever cheat on you."

That warmed my heart. "I'm going to kiss you later for saying that." We'd had enough PDA on TV.

"I look forward to it." Jake wagged his brows.

I hoped after the office scene that was it for me and Jake on the show, but that was wishful thinking. The next scene was of Vivian watching the footage of our makeup scene with the other wives. She cried, like big fat tears. Meanwhile, Elsie and Marla were discussing how much they liked me, and Heather was talking about my line of clothing. They even showed my website and some of my designs. That wasn't so bad. I should have known it wouldn't end all nice like that.

Vivian didn't appreciate how the spotlight had shifted to me or how all the wives were telling her to let the Jake thing go. They were all quite impressed with our kiss. Like I said, the Baldwin brothers knew their stuff. Which, unfortunately, Vivian knew all about, as she and Jake had made out at Love Circle back in high school. I didn't want to think about it. I had a feeling, though, that she had always remembered it.

Vivian stood, tall and proud wearing a skintight leopard-print dress. Did she show houses in that? The better question was if she ever worked. She wiped her eyes. "You can all think what you want, but in my heart, I know the truth. And the truth is that Jake loves

119

me and the only reason he married Kasie was because she tricked him into getting her pregnant."

I popped up out of my seat. How dare she say something like that. I held my stomach, sick.

Momma swore at the TV.

Several of our friends booed.

Jake stood next to me. "Baby, don't let her get to you."

"Why is it always the girl's fault?" my voice shook on the verge of tears.

"You know as well as I do that's not what happened between us. And not for one second have I ever thought that way," Jake tried to comfort me.

"Yeah, but it's what the world always thinks. No one ever thinks about the girl."

Pam and Rich, my in-laws, both looked my way, a little red in the face. They knew very well they had said some of the same things as Vivian. Things that had hurt and that I'd lived with for years.

I tuned back to the TV. Marla sneered at Vivian. "You need to stop making trouble for them. I saw them together. They're obviously in love."

Vivian laughed maniacally. "You doubt me?"

Elsie stepped back from her as if she were afraid. "Vivian, you're married. Let them be," she said bravely.

Vivian held her hand up to the ceiling as if she were a pastor and about to call down the heavens. I think she was reaching the wrong way. The woman was the devil herself. "With God as my witness, I won't stop until the truth is known."

They went to a commercial.

Jake was furious and turned off the TV.

We all just stared at each other, stunned for a moment. Abs finally broke the silence. "At least we know with God as her witness, she's done for. She's going to need witness protection after this."

Everyone laughed except me and Jake.

Jake wrapped his arm around me. "All that matters is that we know the truth."

I wasn't so sure about that. I had a feeling our lives were about to get even more interesting.

Chapter Thirteen

JAKE TURNED SOME GEORGE Strait on the surround sound before wrapping his arms around me from behind while I stood at the sink rinsing off dishes. Our guests had all left.

"Baby, the dishes can wait." He nuzzled my ear.

Even as upset as I still was over that stupid show, Jake was getting to me. Shivers went down my entire body. "You're not playing fair. You know what George does to me." George was another egg popper and partly to blame for me getting pregnant. George and Jake were a lethal combination.

"Believe me, I know," he groaned in my ear.

I half-heartedly tried to push him away, but he wasn't having it. "Kasie, dance with me."

"You don't like to dance."

"I do with you. Please." He reached over and turned off the water before turning me toward him.

I rested my head against his chest and sighed. "How did this become our lives? I'm never going to be able to leave the house." Not to say the craziness wasn't going to find me here. My website had already exploded with new orders, which was great. With that came a lot of well wishes and messages about how adorable Jake and I were together. Although, it wasn't all roses and sunshine. One crazy lady wrote me saying I should be ashamed of myself for keeping Jake and Vivian apart. She said there was a word for women like me—slut. I'd heard it before, but it had been a while. Regardless, it still stung.

Jake kissed my head while his hands glided down my back. His warm hands dived under my shirt, and he pressed his fingers against my back, drawing me closer. The feel of his skin against mine made my body come to life. His touch had a magic of its own. A magical way of making clothes fall off.

"Don't tempt me, Jake. If we make love now, I'll never know the truth."

He leaned away with concern in his baby blues. "Please don't tell me you believe Vivian."

"It's not her. It's us. For a long time, Jake," I choked up, "I've felt like your regret. That I was the consolation prize or maybe even the white elephant gift."

"Kasie."

I could hear the pain in his voice.

His hands made their way out of my shirt and cupped my face. "I have had regrets. Yes. You are not one of them. Kasie," he said tenderly, "you were my dream girl. From the first day I saw you the summer before our senior year, I wanted you. I wanted you so bad, I lost my head. Every time we were together, I promised myself I wouldn't let it go too far. But I wanted to. Then, that night happened, and I pushed it further than I ever had, and when you didn't stop me, I selfishly lived out my fantasy. And kept living it out every time we were together, without thinking about the consequences for you or me. I couldn't get enough of you."

"I felt the same way, and you didn't do anything I didn't want you to do. We both lived out our fantasies all those nights." Tears leaked out of my eyes and fell like raindrops on his strong hands.

"Then, the consequences came with two pink lines. I felt like a ton of bricks had been dropped on me. I was so scared; I didn't know how to feel. The only thing I could feel was guilt. You were so sick, all because of me. I wanted to take care of you, but I didn't know how I could. The decisions we made after that seemed like a blur. I never stopped to think. I was just trying to get by and provide for you and Maribelle. It wasn't until later that I . . ."

"Had regrets," I finished for him.

He hung his head. "Yes. I hated my job and started to envy other people's success, especially people we knew. I started to resent my life."

"You resented me," I stuttered, my heart aching.

"No. Yes," he whispered, shame lacing his words. "I feel like such a bastard saying that." His hands dropped.

"I'd rather know the truth. Because in my heart, I already knew you . . . you . . ." I started blubbering and couldn't say the words.

He took my hand and held it between us, his own eyes watering. "Kasie Ann, I'm sorry. It wasn't really you I resented."

"You just said you d . . . did," I stammered.

"Because it was easier that way; but when you left, I realized it wasn't you. I knew then I hadn't given up anything until I let you walk out the door." He reached up and his thumb gently brushed some of my tears. "Kasie, after we started dating, nothing else mattered as much as you. You filled me in ways I didn't even know existed. Then you gave me Maribelle, and she took ahold of me. I know I made mistakes and had no idea what the hell I was doing. You both consumed me, and as hard as it was, I couldn't imagine my life without either one of you. But as time went on and disappointments piled up, I began to think, what if."

"What if I'd never ruined your life?"

He grabbed my shirt and pulled me to him. "No, Kasie." His hot breath brushed over my skin. "Please don't talk like that."

"Just tell me the truth, Jake," I begged.

"You want to know the truth?" His eyes gazed so deeply into my own, I could feel them touch my soul. "The truth is, I want you. I need you. I love you." His lips played above my own. "You are better than any dream. I'm sorry I forgot that for a while. But the God's honest truth is, reality with you is better than anything I ever dreamed up."

My heart fluttered and hope flared. Those were the most beautiful words I had ever heard. "I want to believe you."

He brushed my lips with his own. "I promise to do whatever I can to make you believe in me again." He pressed a kiss to my lips. "Dance with me."

I rested my head on his chest and he wrapped his

arms around me. We barely swayed to the crooning of the greatest singer of all time. For a moment, I enjoyed the protection of his arms while I silently prayed we could work things out. That we would never regret or resent one another. Then, I remembered something.

"Jake, what were you going to tell me earlier in the kitchen? What is it that you want?"

He pulled me closer. "For now, only you."

"But—"

"Baby, I promise to tell you later. I need to work on a few things first."

"Like what?"

"You'll see."

There were a lot of things to see. But mostly it was my sewing machine and room. I'd had so many orders, I had to stop taking them. Even with Momma helping when she could and Abs quitting her job to work with me full time, there were too many. I mean, that was great, except I felt like I was drowning in fabric and the spotlight. Tera was relentless. Apparently, Jake and I were a big hit. She wanted us to do our own show—*Kasie and Jake at Home.* Yeah, well, Kasie and Jake weren't sharing a home right now. Not to say Jake wasn't here every second he could be. However, I didn't want to be the girl who so many people thought had trapped Jake. If only they could have seen how terrified I'd been when those two lines had appeared. My life had changed in an instant. I'd gone from being excited about prom, to knowing another life was solely dependent on me. Regardless, I needed to know that Jake truly saw that our reality was better than our dreams. And we were absolutely not doing our own reality show.

Unfortunately, I wasn't quite done with reality TV. Like I said, Tera was relentless and held the whole getting arrested thing over my head. Though Jake didn't think she had a leg to stand on. Either way, I told her I would let her film me one more time when Elsie and Marla came over for their fittings. After that, I was done, and if she ever came back, I would release the "security" footage on my social media pages and the pictures Abs had taken of Vivian's closet. That seemed to tame the beast. Hopefully.

I wasn't sure what could be done about the other beast, Vivian. I feared for what she would say on the next episode. There were literally people out there making Vivian and Jake shirts. One vendor on Etsy was making shirts that said *Free Jake*. Like I was keeping him hostage. Y'all, the lady was married and obviously insane. Poor Beau. Speaking of Beau or X, I had written to him to apologize for getting caught. I was waiting for his response.

Meanwhile, I was sewing away and listening to Abs ramble about the merits of Dallas. Then she hit me with a question that made me fear for her.

Abs had sewn the last stitch on a camisole bodice when she looked over her sewing machine at me. "Do you think Dallas would ever consider settling down?"

I was so startled by her question, my seam zigzagged. I stopped sewing before I did more damage to the jumpsuit I was working on and looked up at her.

She wore a look of trepidation and was biting her lip and blinking her eyes repeatedly.

"Well . . . um . . . maybe. I mean, I love Dallas, but he's kind of gotten around. Do you want to be with someone like that?"

She let out the deepest of sighs. "I know I shouldn't, but there's something about him."

"Baldwin men are intoxicating, but they can be maddening too."

She sat back in her chair and took a long sip of Coke. She wasn't even bothering with diet today. "I know I shouldn't get sucked in, but I can't stop thinking about him."

I stood and went over to her. I knelt next to her chair and took her hand like she was a patient in a hospital. She had Baldwin sickness; it was real and possibly incurable. "Abs, maybe you should stop seeing him."

She stared up to the tray ceiling. "I probably should, but I don't want to. He makes me feel alive in a way I never have. And treats me so good when we're together."

"Yeah, that's how they get you," I commiserated with her.

She lowered her chin. "I mean, you and Jake have been married for a long time."

"Yes, but it hasn't been easy, and we aren't even living together."

"You will be soon. I can feel it. No marriage is ever easy."

"Abs, just take it slow with Dallas. I don't want you to get hurt."

"Oh, sugar, if you aren't willing to get hurt, you're never going to have love—at least not the real thing."

I sunk to the floor, letting what she said sink in. "Well then, I say go for it."

She narrowed her eyes at me but smiled. "Are you going for it too?"

"We've made it this far, right? No one ever thought we would."

She tugged on my ponytail. "You prove the world wrong. Anyone who would doubt you is a fool."

"I might be a fool," I admitted. I'd been doubting myself a lot lately. You know, except when I broke into Vivian's house and went on a national TV show.

"No. Jake was the fool. You're cautious, as you should be, but cautious people never change the world, nor do they have amazing love stories."

"How do I know if Jake has really changed?"

"Honey, he didn't really need to change; he just needed to remember. And the only way you can know if his memory is fully intact is to try. And I would say you already both are."

"Yeah, we are," I whispered.

"I want to try with Dallas too," she eeked out.

I swallowed down my cautious words and only said, "I wish you all the best."

"I wish the same for you."

Me too. Me too.

Chapter Fourteen

I APPRECIATE YOUR KIND words. No apology is necessary. I just hated to see a relationship end when it didn't need to. I hope you and your husband can work things out. A word of caution, though: Vivian will not give up easily. She doesn't like to lose and can hold a grudge longer than anyone I know. She's a ruthless businessperson and knows how to play the game. Be smart and don't play it.

X

Beau's words sent shivers down my spine. I had read his message several times this morning while I was getting ready. Ready for my last brush with fame, I hoped.

The doorbell rang and I groaned. The crew of *Wives of Nashville* was early. I needed more Diet Coke. I walked toward the door at a turtle's pace, not wanting to answer it. Smoothing out my form-fitting white cardigan, I opened the door. The person standing on my porch was not who I'd expected.

My mother-in-law, Pam, stood there looking like she'd rather be anywhere else. No surprise there. She pulled her wool coat around her tighter. "Kasie, I, uh . . . would like to speak with you," she stammered.

This probably didn't bode well for me, but I opened the door farther. "Come on in," I said against my better judgment. Pam was a severe-looking woman with gray spiky hair and amber hawk eyes that zeroed in on me.

"I can take your coat and make some coffee," I offered.

She waved her hand in the air. "Not necessary. I won't be long."

I leaned against the nearest wall in the foyer, bracing myself for her assault and trying to think what I had done lately to tick her off. Maybe it was all the negative attention Jake was getting, or maybe she was upset we were trying to work it out. Who knew?

She cleared her throat and looked down at her penny loafers. "I feel like I owe you an apology."

I popped off the wall. *What? Did I hear her right?*

She braved looking at me while heavily exhaling. "What you said the other night about blaming women and girls, it shamed me. I thought about Maribelle and how I would wish for her to be treated. I thought about how Rich and I treated you over the years, and especially when you were younger." She swallowed hard. "It wasn't right. And I'm . . . sorry," she said with difficulty.

Wow. Like so wow I didn't know what to say. I just stared in amazement at her.

"You have shown grace and been a fearless mother and wife despite it all. Admittedly, you have

131

been more than my son probably deserved at times. For that, I thank you."

I didn't need her thanks, though it was nice to hear it. "I've always loved Jake."

"I know. I'm sorry we ever said that you didn't know what love was. You proved we were the ones who didn't." She spun on her heels and reached for the door.

"Pam," I called out before she could go. "I would like it if we could be friends."

"I would like that too." She opened the door and escaped like the house was on fire, shutting the door as she went.

I stared at the door, wondering what had just happened. Unfortunately, I couldn't contemplate too long. The wicked witch arrived on her broomstick. Thankfully, Marla and Elsie came too. As crazy as I thought those ladies were, I had to admit, I was beginning to really like them. Even if they pouted their lips like teenage girls and wore shoes that cost more than my car. And despite the fact they were wearing *Team Kasie and Jake* T-shirts to my house—in pink, of course, with lots of hearts floating around our names.

I smiled at them while shaking my head. "Good morning, ladies." Meaning Marla and Elsie. Tera was more like a hyena, and not the laughing kind.

"Do you love our new shirts?" Marla laughed. "They are all the rage."

"Seriously, they are flying off the shelves," Elsie squealed and clapped her hands.

"We brought you some." Marla reached into her

large designer bag, pulled out a few shirts, and handed them to me.

I reluctantly took them. This was the south, where we monogrammed everything, yet it seemed weird to wear a shirt with my name on it. "Thank you. I think."

"Oh, you'll be thanking us," Tera butted in and pushed her way past Elsie and Marla to get inside. My house instantly felt like it was in need of a biblical cleansing.

I was grateful that Abs showed up at the same time with a 64-ounce Diet Coke for me from the local convenience store. Bless her and bless caffeine.

I let everyone, including the production crew, back to my sewing room. It was a light and airy room with touches of Jake everywhere. I particularly loved the built-in window benches he had made me. I had sewn the paisley pillows that rested on them.

"Ooh, this is a darling room," Elsie gushed.

"Thank you. Jake built a lot of it."

"I love a good handyman, if you get what I mean." Marla nudged me.

I was sure I got what she meant.

I set my new T-shirts on one of the tables before I pointed to the dress and jumpsuit on my mannequins. "Those are for you ladies."

"Don't say that yet," Tera scolded me. "We need their real reactions."

"Is there anything real about your show?" I couldn't help but ask.

Marla, Abs, and Elsie snickered.

Tera lasered in on me with her soulless eyes. "My paycheck," she snarled.

I rolled my eyes and ignored her. I was so happy to be done with her after today.

Once the lighting and cameras were set up, I was able to really show Elsie and Marla their outfits. Abs worked with Marla, and I with Elsie, taking the measurements we needed to make the ensembles perfect fits for our famous clients.

Marla and Elsie were overly complimentary about their new pieces of clothing. Unfortunately, like my life always seemed to go, with the good came the bad.

Marla stepped off the raised platform and did a spin in the middle of the room. The strappy silver-and-black-bodiced evening gown with its brocade skirt was stunning, if I did say so myself.

"Y'all are going on the map with this one," Marla commented.

"I'm happy you love it." I stuck my last pin through the hem of Elsie's pink pantsuit that she was absolutely giddy about.

"I can't wait to wear this to the botanical garden gala in April. Vivian is going to flip her lid," Marla sang.

I'd been hoping the V-word wouldn't be brought up.

Elsie hopped off the platform. "You better watch out for her," she warned me. "She hasn't been very nice this week."

"When is she ever nice?" Marla deadpanned.

"Well . . . she was a couple of times." Elsie had to think a little too hard. Then she grabbed my hand. "I fear for your safety. She really thinks you stole Jake from her."

I stood upright and stretched my back. I doubted that's what she really thought, even so she was going to play it for all it was worth. After all, Jake was only a car salesman, as she'd put it. Regardless, I was going to speak my truth. "That's not true. Jake broke a date off with her in high school. That's it. End of story. In fact, I was always jealous of her growing up because she was gorgeous and popular. Then she went on to be incredibly successful. It's sad she can't stop and look at her own life and realize how good she has it."

Everyone seemed to be staring at me.

"What?" I asked, feeling self-conscious.

"The way she talks about you, it makes it seem like there was a huge rivalry and you were out to get her," Marla responded.

I spat out a laugh. "Nothing could be further from the truth. The only reason we were in the same school is because they'd rezoned the area I lived in due to it being so poor. And Jake didn't move in until the summer before our senior year. Regardless, Vivian always made sure I knew my place, and it was well below her. Not to mention, while everyone was off celebrating graduation, I was puking my guts out and getting ready to have a small wedding in my parents' backyard. I didn't have time to be out to get anyone. And believe me, she made sure to rub it in my face about what I was missing out on and how I'd ruined my life and Jake's." I tried to keep the emotion out of my voice.

Elsie hugged me. "You didn't ruin anyone's life. As far as I can tell, you did real good."

"Hell yeah, she did," Abs threw in.

I blushed from the attention. "Well, I'd like to think we did okay. It's sad Vivian can't feel the same about her life."

Marla nodded. "Sometimes I think when life comes too easy, you never appreciate it. You can never satisfy your appetite. And the only way for Vivian to feel good about herself is to make others feel bad. Which is why I still plan on exposing her." Marla wagged her brows.

I didn't even want to know how. The less I knew, the better. "Let's not talk about her," I suggested. I hated knowing this was all being recorded. But I had said the truth and hoped people would listen.

"Yes," Marla agreed. "I get too much of her on a daily basis."

I hoped that was it for filming, but Jake made an unexpected visit. He popped his handsome head in. "Hey, baby." He sounded uneasy.

All eyes and cameras went to him.

He tugged on his dress shirt collar. "I thought you would be done by now."

I pranced over to him and pulled him inside. Might as well.

He grimaced before holding out a white paper bag that smelled like cinnamon and all things wonderful. "You've been working like crazy, so I thought I would drop off your favorite muffins." He'd been so thoughtful lately. He'd basically supplied all my meals the last several days and gave foot rubs and back rubs that had almost led to the mixing of grits, though instead we'd ended up talking for hours and being intimate in the way we needed to be right now.

"You're the best." I kissed his lips. I turned toward everyone else. "Is that a wrap?" Please let it be.

Tera's eyes lit up like an evil warlord as she neared us. I suddenly felt like a fly trapped in a web, and the spider was closing in on its juicy meal.

I backed up against Jake, who wrapped an arm around me.

"We aren't quite done," Tera hissed. "Our viewers can't get enough of you two. Your kiss made head-lines."

I cringed thinking about some of the local coverage that kiss had gotten. There was even a clip of it that had been made into memes. They were calling it "doing a Jasie." Apparently, that was our couple name.

"The question is"—Tera slid closer— "how can we get more of you?"

"You can't," I was quick to say, while Jake said, "I have an idea."

My head whipped toward him so fast I probably needed a chiropractor. "Jake?"

"Can I get a minute with my wife?"

We were going to need lots of minutes. Lots and lots.

Chapter Fifteen

JAKE AND I WALKED hand in hand down Fifth Avenue in downtown Nashville that night, past a large crowd waiting to get into the Ryman, the Mother Church of Country Music, for a concert. The acoustics were amazing, and you sat in pews, not seats. It was already dark and cold, and people were standing in clusters trying to keep warm, yet that didn't stop a group of women from rushing us and flashing us their Team Kasie and Jake shirts. Was this really our life?

"Will you please take a picture with us?" an exuberant brunette begged.

Her phone was out before we could even reply. Before I knew it, we were in a thousand selfies.

"Y'all are the cutest things ever," another woman gushed.

Some other woman shouted at us from across the street. "Homewreckers!"

Excuse me? How could we be homewreckers?

Jake whisked me away after that. I had to say, I was a bit annoyed with him. We were out in public because he had to show me why he was considering

Tera's offer to do our own show. He'd promised me I wouldn't be disappointed, but that was all he would say about it other than to beg me to trust him.

We moved quickly up the street a couple more blocks before we turned the corner. There were clear signs of renovation going on with the brick buildings that lined the narrow street. Scaffolding and dust lined the sidewalk. A couple of attractive-looking business-men waited outside an empty boarded-up storefront with a filthy glass door.

One of the men approached us. "You must be Mr. and Mrs. Baldwin. I'm Christopher McKay, and this is my partner, Charles Beckett, but you can call him Beck."

"A pleasure to meet you," Beck crooned with an English accent. Oh my. It was then that I recognized him. His wife, Call, was a famous country singer. They were local celebrities. Which made it even more confusing that we were meeting him and his partner. Jake and I were only temporarily famous—more like infamous.

"Nice to meet you." Jake shook each man's hand. "Call me Jake. This is my lovely wife, Kasie."

I shook both their hands as well, still confused.

"Why don't we step out of the cold," Christopher suggested, "and take a look at the property."

I looked at Jake, who was smiling like the Cheshire cat. "What is this?"

"You'll see." He sounded more excited than when the Predators had made it to the Stanley Cup finals a few years ago.

We walked into what looked like an abandoned

building with broken boarded-up windows and pieces of wood lying all over the dusty floor. The walls were exposed, and the high wood-beam ceilings looked a bit rotted.

"I know it doesn't look like much now," Christopher smiled at us, "but with some love and work, this place would be a gem."

Gem? I was thinking more like cubic zirconia.

"It's in a prime location," Beck added. "A bakery is going in next door, and the foot traffic here is unbeatable. The perfect place for a boutique."

I leaned into Jake. "You see Maribelle and Me here?" I was so taken aback.

He ran a cold finger down my cheek. "I see you all over this place."

Suddenly, the old building looked more like a possibility than a disaster area. I could see racks of clothes, a beautiful display window, round shelves in the middle filled with accessories. And even fitting rooms.

But before I could get too far into my lovely vision, I whispered for Jake's ears only, "We can't afford a place like this." Even though it was a wreck, nothing downtown was cheap. Especially this close to Music Row.

"We could if . . ."

I let out a huge breath and bit my lip. Before I could say anything, though, Christopher and Beck were giving us the sales pitch of a lifetime. We walked around every square inch of the place while they described its attributes and, of course, the cost. I think I vomited in my mouth some when they threw out the figure like it was a bargain or something. Dazed and even dazzled, I took pictures with my phone of everything while my mind swirled with the possibility.

While I contemplated basically selling my soul, I took peeks at Jake, who intently listened and made notes in his phone of everything Christopher and Beck were saying. I couldn't help but fall more in love with him. The fact that he had even gone to the trouble of finding this place spoke volumes to me.

When the tour was over, Christopher and Beck left us with their cards and told us to call with any questions. Oh, I had questions—lots of them.

Jake and I were silent for a moment after we were left alone to stare at the old brick building. It had so much character. I could envision myself coming here every day. I wanted it so badly it almost hurt. But did I want it enough to give up my privacy? Well, what I had left of it, anyway.

"Let's take a walk," Jake suggested.

"I don't want to be seen by anyone."

"Baby, it doesn't matter where we go right now, that's going to happen. I, for one, am proud to show you off."

I playfully smacked his coat-covered chest. "Okay. Where are we going?"

"You'll see."

"It's not another astronomically expensive place, is it?" I teased.

"Well, it is, but we're not going to buy it."

"I don't think we can buy this place." I pointed at my would-be dream.

Jake put his finger to my lips. "Shhh. Follow me."

My interest was piqued as we walked toward Music Square. There were plenty of gawkers, but no one stopped us. Thankfully, it was chilly enough that most people wanted to dart inside to the warmth of a restaurant or bar. I barely felt the cold as I was thinking. Lots of thinking.

After a good brisk walk, Jake placed me in front of one of the most historic buildings in all of Nashville—RCA Studio A. The large brown brick-and-stone building with the iconic dog and phonograph sign stood majestic and stoic. It had been saved from being turned into condos several years back, to the delight of every Nashville citizen.

"Why are we here?" I asked.

Jake looked up to the top of the building. "Baby, some of the biggest legends of country music recorded here—Dolly Parton and Willie Nelson. What would the world be without 'Jolene'?"

I did love that song, even if it was about a cheating man. "It is a great song, but what does that have to do with us?"

Jake turned me toward him and gazed into my eyes, which were watering from the cold but warmed by his tender look. "Kasie, you asked me what it was I wanted. What I want more than anything is to make your dreams come true."

Tears leaked out of my eyes and dripped down my cheeks. Oh man, did I love him. "Jake, it's so expensive."

"It is. But"—he pointed to the building— "think about the sacrifices made in this building to make dreams come true. I bet most everyone who has walked the hallowed halls of this studio would agree it was worth it, as hard as it was."

"Yes, but I don't want to give you up. People who do shows like the one Tera is proposing frequently break up. I'm not willing to take that risk."

Jake thought for a moment. "We're stronger than that."

"Are we? We don't even live under the same roof right now."

Jake tugged on my coat and drew me closer. "I want to change that. Kasie, I don't want to spend another lonely night away from you ever again. I want to see your face first thing in the morning, and I want you to be the last thing I see at night." He rested his forehead against mine. His minty breath filled my senses. "I want to make love to you and have a baby with you."

I leaned away, stunned. "A b . . . baby," I stuttered. That had escalated quickly.

His thumb brushed away a few tears. "Yes, Kasie Ann. When I said I wanted to make your dreams come true, I meant all of them."

"But . . . our baby is grown up, and we're old." Not like really old, but it seemed late in the game to start over.

"You're still the girl who lights my world on fire. You are the one I love and the one I want to be with."

Those words filled my soul in a way nothing else could. It was as if Jake was the sun and he melted every doubt I'd ever had. I knew then that I wasn't the "love the one you're with" woman. I knew something else too. "Jake, let's go home."

Chapter Sixteen

I WOKE UP WHERE I had longed to be, in the comfort of Jake's arms, my head on his bare chest. The chest I had watched over the years go from smooth and hairless to defined with a forest of dark curls. I looked up and admired his long, lush eyelashes and the curve of his red lips, still swollen from the workout they'd received throughout the night. His tight jawline and angular cheeks still made my heart pitter-patter. And that messy curly hair would always do me in.

While I admired my husband and reveled in being so close to him, I thought about what he had proposed last night. I loved him so much for being willing to do something I knew we would both hate, just so I could have my own storefront. Yet the sacrifice didn't seem like a good trade-off. Wasn't a sacrifice supposed to be giving something up to gain something better? This moment, our reconciliation, was better than anything. I wasn't willing to risk that, not for the world. My world slumbered peacefully next to me and in Tuscaloosa. We would find another way to fund the boutique.

About the other dream Jake had spoken of. Oh. Wow. That was huge. We would literally be starting over again. How would Maribelle feel about that? And I didn't want people to think we were having a baby to fix our marriage. Did I really want to be up all night? So, I was basically up all last night—we had a lot of making up to do—but did I want to be up all night every night for months? However, the thought of a sweet baby with curly strawberry blonde hair popped into my head. I could still feel the way Maribelle felt in my arms, and I could smell her sweet, intoxicating scent, a mixture of lavender and baby powder. I ached to experience that again. To snuggle a baby against my chest and nurse her. To watch Jake bounce her and coo at her or rock her to sleep.

It was a big decision, though. A life-altering one.

I made circles with my finger on Jake's chest. As weird as it sounded, I missed him and wanted him to wake up. I wanted to face the day with him—together.

It didn't take long for his eyes to flutter open. The light of the sun was filtering in through the shades and illuminated his handsome face.

"Good morning," he whispered; his voice had that morning croak.

I felt the rumble of his words in his chest. "Best morning."

His hand glided down my bare arm. "Last night was amazing."

I trembled just thinking of it. "It was." I snuggled in closer to him, breathing in his musky scent mixed with my floral-smelling perfume. It was the perfect blend. "Jake, I've been thinking."

"What about?"

"The building, the offer, the stupid show, a baby."

"That's a lot, darlin'." He chuckled.

"It is." I propped myself up on his chest so I could peer into his sleepy baby blues. "So, here's what I'm thinking. We say no to the show—"

"But it will finance the—"

I pressed my lips to his. "Shhh."

"Mmm. Feel free to shush me anytime." He took a small taste before his lips glided off mine.

"So." I smiled. "No show. We would both be miserable. Though I love you so much for being willing. We can find another way. I know we can. Maybe do a smaller place and a cheaper location, like Franklin."

Jake thought for a moment. "Hmm. We could possibly make that work if I did most of the labor."

"Well, now that you brought that up, I think you should quit your job."

His brow popped.

"I'm serious. You're unhappy working for your uncle, and I'm going to be making a lot of money for the next few months. And we have some money saved up. You'll have plenty of time to look for something else. Something that makes you feel happy and not trapped or resentful."

"Kasie, I told you I didn't and don't resent you."

"And I believe you, but you do resent your uncle and your job."

He nodded, reluctantly.

"Jake, you deserve to have your dreams come true too."

"They did last night," he groaned.

It was definitely dreamy, but we couldn't live our lives in bed, as fantastic as it was. "Yes, that was wonderful, and I'm willing to make your dreams come true again this morning." I flashed him a sexy smile. "But first, I need to know if you were serious about having another baby."

He pulled me to him. "Yes. We can start right now."

I popped back up. "Hold on, tiger. What I meant was, do you really want another baby? And not just because I want one."

He brushed back my sleep-tangled hair. A tender look washed over him. "Kasie, I'm not going to lie, it makes me nervous. The last time we had a baby, it scared the hell out of me."

"Me too," I whispered. But it hadn't scared me off. In a lot of ways, it had empowered me. And I'd ached to have another baby—actually lots of babies.

"But," he said, "I loved watching you being a momma and love our kid. I figure we did pretty good the first go-around. It would be a shame not to try again."

"You realize our lives will never be the same."

"Kasie, you rocked my world a long time ago. I never want to go back."

That sealed the deal. My lips fell on his. "Let's make a baby."

"Hold that thought," he whispered against my lips.

I leaned away, concerned. "I thought you wanted to—"

He flashed me a sexy grin. "Believe me, I definitely want to, but I want to give you something first. We're going to do it the right way this time."

The right way?

He hopped out of bed, grabbed his jeans, and reached into his pocket for something that he kept concealed in his closed hand. I sat up and pulled the sheet up around me, curious.

He crawled back under the covers with me, grinning from ear to ear. When he opened his hand, I knew exactly why. I burst into tears, staring at my wedding ring, which now had a definite upgrade. The small diamond had been replaced with what looked like a round one-carat diamond.

"Oh, Jake. It's beautiful."

"I thought it was about time I made good on my promise to you. I love you, Kasie Ann. Will you be my wife and the momma to my babies?"

"Yes. A thousand times yes," I choked out.

He took my hand and slipped on the beautiful ring. Then he leaned in and brushed my lips with his own. "Now, where were we?"

We were right where I wanted to be.

"This is going to be the last time we watch this show," I declared to all my family and friends from the comfort of Jake's arms on the love seat.

"That's what you said last time, Momma," Maribelle reminded me.

I couldn't help but stare at my baby girl. She was

sitting next to Rhett, who was home for a few days from school, so she'd driven up to see him. It was like a flashback of her daddy and me. Except Rhett was all sorts of blond. Still, he gave Maribelle the same look Jake used to give me. Honestly, the one he still gave me. It said, *you're the one I love.* I tried not to worry about it. Maribelle had a good head on her shoulders, and she was the feistiest thing I'd ever known. She would reach her goals and become a pediatric nurse, of that I had no doubt.

I noticed my husband also kept glancing their way.

"She'll be okay," I whispered.

"She reminds me so much of you at that age. That boy has no chance."

I snuggled in closer to him, ready to be done with reality TV forever. The only reason I was even watching it tonight was because Marla and Elsie had made me promise to tune in. Jake and I were actually old news. Apparently, Tera was miffed we wouldn't take her up on her offer for our own show, so we'd become an off-limits topic for the last few weeks. Praise. Even Vivian hadn't mentioned Jake. Reconciling with Beau was her new way to gain sympathy. She'd even made Team Vivian and Beau shirts for everyone last week and called him pookie bear at every turn, which you could tell he hated. All the other wives had laughed at her and refused to wear the T-shirts.

Tera's other motive for keeping us off the show was that she didn't want Jake and me to financially gain any more than we already had from our unwelcome brush with fame. Little did she know, my orders were still skyrocketing, and I had been approached with a deal I couldn't refuse.

"Everyone, settle down," Abs yelled. She was still in love with the show. And I was pretty sure she was in love with Dallas too. They were sitting on the floor with her between his legs, leaning against him. They looked so cozy and at ease with each other. Jake had tried to get Dallas to tell him if he saw this as a long-term thing, but Dallas refused to say anything other than that he was enjoying himself. Clearly, they were very hands-on.

The show started with all the wives in Vivian's blindingly white kitchen. Vivian was prancing around in some booty shorts and a red V-neck sweater. Did she ever work?

Elsie was wearing the pink jumpsuit I'd made her. Vivian glared at it like it had personally killed her grandmother or something.

Marla was sitting on the countertop, flipping through some pictures and evilly smiling. I wondered what that was all about.

"So," Marla drawled. "I'm venturing into the world of fashion."

Elsie giggled while all the other wives gave her their attention.

"Oh really?" Vivian sounded skeptical. "Honey, aren't you a little old? I would hate for you to embarrass yourself."

Marla jumped off the counter. "Thank you for your concern. Though I think my little boutique, Maribelle and Me, is going to be all the rage in Nashville."

Hoots and hollers erupted in our family room. Yep, Marla wanted to go into business with me. She had invested in the property downtown, with a little help from Beau. Something I knew, via Marla, he had kept from Vivian.

"I love that line of clothes," Elsie declared.

Vivian turned a shade of puce. "Ugh, I guess if you like the sweet look."

Elsie surprised me and smirked. "Yes, ma'am, I do."

I loved that girl. Loved her enough that I'd agreed to do her husband's music video with Maribelle. The money was all going toward Maribelle's education so Jake and I could focus on our new venture of becoming business owners. I couldn't wait to see him doing all that manual labor. It really melted my butter, as my momma would say.

Speaking of Momma, I think she'd made peace with Jake's and my reconciliation. She'd told him last week she was proud of the man he was becoming. Not sure I'd ever seen Jake beam brighter.

Maybe not as bright as Marla was beaming. She kept staring intently at the pictures she was holding, going through them and smiling. I was so curious to see what they were.

"Well," Vivian directed the attention back to herself, as always. "All I know is, I wouldn't be caught dead in any of *her* clothes."

Marla's eyes lit up as if Vivian had said the magic words. "Yes, I do suppose they are a bit tame for your taste, Velvet Kitty," she purred.

Vivian dropped the glass of water she had just

picked up. It shattered in a hundred pieces against the white tile floor. "What d ... did you call me?" she stammered.

Marla spread all the pictures she had been looking at out across the island like a blackjack dealer. "Looks like you were such a naughty little kitty."

The camera zeroed in on the pictures, which featured Vivian dressed like a stripper, right down to her barely-there blue velvet bikini that matched her bed's headboard, and her perky velvet kitty ears and matching eye mask. Meow.

"I knew she was too good during that pole-dancing episode." I laughed, flabbergasted by this turn of events. I couldn't fathom why she had been a stripper, but truth was often stranger than fiction.

Vivian was trying to snatch the pictures away, but all the other wives grabbed them first and began examining them. She began screaming and crying. "Those aren't me."

"Sure looks like you." Heather held up a picture to the light. "I can even see the strawberry-shaped birthmark near your bellybutton. When was this?"

"Never!" Vivian shouted.

Marla laughed sardonically. "Oh please, honey; Kirk Cannon, the owner of the strip club in Orlando, totally recognized you. Said you were a bad, bad kitty back in the day."

"Didn't you go to college in Florida?" Elsie asked.

Vivian was spluttering and trying to stand in front of the cameras. "Shut it off. Shut it off," she cried.

They went to commercial, and everyone at our house erupted into fits of giggles.

"Hello Kitty. I didn't see that coming." I was completely stunned. And admittedly happier than I probably should have been about it.

"I hope you never have any doubts now about my choice, the only choice there ever was for me," Jake whispered in my ear.

I turned to face him. Such love lived in his eyes. I felt it in my soul. "Jake Baldwin, you're my choice."

"Are you saying you love the one you're with?" he half teased me.

"Always and forever." I wasn't teasing one bit.

Epilogue

One Year Later

"I CAN'T BELIEVE THIS is really happening." I stood, awestruck, in front of Maribelle and Me in the spring sun that warmed my heart and soul. The black-and-white striped awning added a touch of class to the storefront, and the planter boxes bursting with green added a touch of life. I brushed my fingers over our logo on the glass door.

Jake chastely kissed me once. "You worked so hard this last year. You deserve this."

I rested my hand on his cheek. "I couldn't have done this without you." Jake had put in some major sweat equity. But he'd never been happier. He loved being his own boss and working together toward a common goal. More than anything, I think that's what I loved about the boutique too—it was something we'd done together.

"Why don't we go in before the circus arrives," Jake suggested.

It was the one thing I wasn't looking forward to

today. Marla was still doing *Wives of Nashville,* and the new producer insisted the store opening be part of the show. Tera was long gone after an anonymous source had leaked the real videos of what had happened with Jake and Vivian. That meant Vivian was out too. There was enough bad publicity over it all that Tera was fired, and Vivian's reputation was tarnished enough that their audience had turned on her. Vivian could also never live down the stripper thing. It wasn't that anyone cared that she had been a stripper, it was that she had made herself out to be above such things and looked down her nose at people who lived those kinds of lives. She had even started claiming she'd had to become a stripper to pay for college. Nobody was buying it, as she'd had a full-ride scholarship and her family had money. Despite her attempts to save herself, it was game over when Beau filed for divorce. I'm not sure where Vivian fled to, but I knew one thing: I would never live in her shadow again. Though I would like to ask her sometime why she felt she lived in mine. Perhaps one day she would learn to love the one she was with—herself. Regardless, this season was still as ridiculous as ever. Admittedly, though, the press would be good for business.

Jake opened the door for me, and we walked in. I wanted my moment alone with him here in this space that felt almost sacred. It was like a dream come to life. As I looked over the racks of clothes filled with our spring line in shades of pastels and whites, my eyes filled with tears of gratitude.

Jake wrapped his arms around me from behind.

His hands landed on my belly. Always my belly. "He's coming along."

"I think his foot is in my rib." I shifted uncomfortably.

Jake knelt next to me. "Be nice to your momma." He kissed my belly.

I ran my hand through Jake's dark curly locks. "I hope little man has your hair."

Jake stood and rested a hand on my cheek. "As long as he has your beautiful soul."

"I can already tell he's going to be ornery." Still, I couldn't wait to meet him. We were all anxious. Even Maribelle, who thought it was going to be weird to have such a younger sibling.

Jake laughed. "That's my boy."

"Oh, he's definitely yours. He's already keeping me up all night." I winked.

Jake grabbed the dress I had specially made for the occasion and pulled me closer. I would be offering it in my new maternity line. It was a pleated midi dress with fluted sleeves in a dusty pink.

"I do my best work at night." His sexy voice still sent shivers down my spine.

"I would agree," I responded breathlessly.

We were about to have a moment until our private party got crashed. Maribelle and Rhett walked in first, followed by Marla and Big D. Momma and Jake's parents trailed behind. Next was Elsie and Owen, with the production crew. Beau and his new girlfriend, Caroline, showed up too. Last but not least were Abs and Dallas, though I'm sure they hadn't meant to come at the same time. They'd broken up over the holidays last year. Dallas didn't feel like he could commit, and Abs had decided she wanted more than to just have fun. The ache between the two was palpable. Dallas was an idiot for letting her go. The weird thing was, I hadn't seen him with another woman, which was unheard of. Abs hadn't dated anyone either. She was still pining for the man. I'd warned her about Baldwin men. Their spell was unbreakable, as far as I could tell.

I wanted to go to Abs, but everyone seemed to want my attention. This was a big day. A day I thought I would never see. Who would have ever thought a TV show would save my marriage and change my life? It was like a dream. No. It was better than that. It was reality.

The End

If you enjoyed *Love the One You're With,* here are some other books by Jennifer Peel that you may enjoy:

My Not So Wicked Stepbrother
All's Fair in Love and Blood
The Sidelined Wife
How to Get Over Your Ex in Ninety Days
Narcissistic Tendencies
Honeymoon for One - A Christmas at the Falls Romance
Trouble in Loveland
Paige's Turn
Best of My Love
Facial Recognition

For a complete list of all her books, check out her Amazon page.
https://www.amazon.com/Jennifer-Peel/e/B00SLRYUEG/

Jennifer Peel is a *USA TODAY* best-selling author who didn't grow up wanting to be a writer—she was aiming for something more realistic, like being the first female president. When that didn't work out, she started writing just before her fortieth birthday. Now, after publishing several award-winning and best-selling novels, she's addicted to typing and chocolate. When she's not glued to her laptop and a bag of Dove dark chocolates, she loves spending time with her family, making daily Target runs, reading, and pretending she can do Zumba.

***

If you enjoyed this book, please rate and review it.
You can also connect with Jennifer on social media:
Facebook
Instagram

To learn more about Jennifer and her books, visit her

website at www.jenniferpeel.com

Made in the USA
Middletown, DE
22 September 2023

39082526R00099